A Beth-Hill Novel:
The Abby Duncan Series,
Novella 1:
By Any Other Name

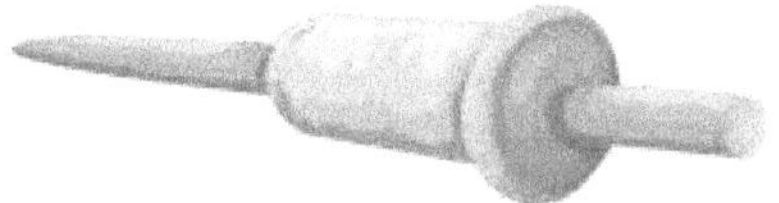

By Jennifer St. Clair

Writers Exchange E-Publishing
http://www.writers-exchange.com

A Beth-Hill Novel: The Abby Duncan Series, Novella 1: By Any Other Name

Copyright 2014, 2015, 2023 Jennifer St. Clair

Writers Exchange E-Publishing

PO Box 372

ATHERTON QLD 4883

Cover Art by: Sandy Cummins and Jatin

Published by Writers Exchange E-Publishing

http://www.writers-exchange.com

Chapter 1

"It's called a phang," Abby said for the twentieth time in an hour. "A supported spindle."

"For what?" the barbarian asked. Or maybe he was supposed to be a Viking; she wasn't quite sure. Vikings weren't exactly welcome in Medieval England--neither were barbarians, for that matter. But the Renaissance Festival had changed a lot since she'd been there last time. More magic and fairies; less historical accuracy.

"For spinning yarn," Abby said, and picked up her demonstration spindle. "Would you like me to show you?"

The barbarian/Viking frowned. "Why would you want to spin your own yarn?"

Abby was just about to go into her spiel when he spotted the glassblower, who was about to give a demonstration. Abandoning fiber for fire, he disappeared, along with her as-yet-only hope for a sale.

Obviously, this wasn't the right venue for spindles or spinning. Perhaps if she'd brought a spinning wheel, someone might be interested, but according to the Powers that Be, spinning wheels weren't period. However, fairy wings evidently were.

Morosely, she sat there and watched as the crowd walked by--completely ignoring both her and her spindles for sale. Perhaps one of the online marketplaces would be better, she thought. Or a fiber festival. Obviously *not* the RenFaire.

"Ooooh, hair sticks!" A girl dressed like an elf--complete with pointed ears--picked up one of the bead spindles, then read the sign in front of it. "'Good for spinning silk'?" She laughed. "Isn't that what spiders do?" Her companion didn't laugh, but looked thoughtful.

And despite the fact that they were *not* hairsticks, at least they bought one after a demonstration.

"Fiber," Abby muttered, and wrote that down in her notebook. "And yarn, too. Why not? Not just spindles; no one knows what to do with them."

Someone darkened the doorway of her tent; she looked up to see what she supposed was a pirate--there were a lot of pirates at the RenFaire this year--dressed in a frock coat that had to be sweltering in the early September heat.

"Spindles," he said thoughtfully. "For spinning yarn."

"Maybe I should have made wands instead," Abby said, half-joking.

"You really expect people to believe--" he looked at her strangely. "How sharp are they? The 'phangs'." He pronounced it wrong, of course, but she was used to that by now.

"The thinner the spinning tip, the longer and faster they spin," Abby said. "They're pretty sharp, but it's really the flicking tip and the balance that makes all the difference. The tip will wear down a little with use, but--"

The pirate picked up one of the phangs and read the tag. "Bloodwood. Hmm. Appropriate, considering the circumstances."

Before Abby could offer a demonstration, he'd pulled out a wad of crumpled bills and peeled off two twenties. Then he looked back at the others, and picked up one more. "Any tax?"

"No, it's included," Abby said. "Would you like a fiber sample to go with your purchase?"

"No thanks," the pirate said, and tucked both phangs into a pocket of his coat. "Have a nice afternoon."

Chapter 2

She sold two more bead spindles ("Hair sticks!") before the fanfare signaled the end of the day. At one point, she had a crowd of three people watching her spin, but not a single one of them purchased anything. While watching the buskers, she wondered if it would help if she put her hat out and sprinkled some coins in it. Maybe that way she'd make back the cost of the booth money.

It took her a little while to pack up her wares; the permanent booth owners could lock up their stock and sleep in the tiny lofts at the top of each fanciful building, but the newer vendors--those with tents--had to tear down each night and set up again the next morning. By the time she'd loaded everything up into her car, the sun had set and most of the faire folk who were staying behind had gathered around the nightly bonfire.

She wasn't quite sure how they managed to keep going all day and still have strength to play music and dance around bonfires at night, but the music was a nice accompaniment as she walked across the quiet grounds to the parking lot.

Okay, *maybe* she'd made a hundred dollars, which barely covered the day's cost of setting up. So far, the RenFaire was an expensive failure of an experiment.

She smiled and nodded to Carmen, who ran the booth next to hers, selling handpainted silk scarves, and maneuvered her wheeled cart down the dirt path, careful not to dump it. She'd done that once before already, embarrassingly enough, and she did not want to do it again.

Carmen's partner Seth--there was another one, named Matt, and they all took shifts as performers as well, apparently--caught up with her right before the gate.

"Would you like some help loading up?" he asked, too nonchalant not to have rehearsed that line; it was the slightly wary look on his face that alerted her to an ulterior motive.

Carmen--along with Grey and Toby, the maskmakers in the booth behind Abby--had rather taken her under their wings. This *was* her first Faire as a vendor, after all, and they had all been very nice to the newbie.

"I'm fine with loading up by myself," she said, "but you can walk with me if you'd like."

"At least let me pull your cart," Seth replied, and she handed off the burden, amused.

They walked in silence through the gate, and then, as they moved up the little hill to the parking lot, Seth asked in a rush, "Are you going to the masquerade tomorrow night?"

The Night Faire was a new addition to the regular Faire program; a masquerade and magic/juggling show that had been sold out for weeks. Tickets were apparently selling online for three times the original cost, and they hadn't been cheap to begin with.

Abby shook her head. "No, I'm not going; I couldn't afford a ticket, and--" she shrugged. "It's kind of pointless to go by myself, isn't it?"

Seth looked away from her. "I thought--if you wanted to go, that is--you might be willing to go with me," he said.

Abby stopped walking and stared at him. He kept going until he realized she'd stopped, and then he turned around.

"But if you don't want to go, that's fine--"

"You have tickets?" she asked, surprised.

Seth smiled. "I live with the juggler," he said. "Well, *we* do. Carmen and Matt and me."

"Carmen and Matt and you--oh," Abby said. "I thought you were--"

"Just friends," Seth said quickly. "Family, really. We're not blood-related, but we've been together for almost eight years now--"

"Did Carmen put you up to this?" Abby asked suspiciously, because Carmen had, perhaps, made some suggestive comments that Abby had chosen to ignore, because she'd thought Carmen and Matt and Seth were *together,* not just partners. And now, there were four of them?

"She threatened to ask you herself," Seth said after a moment. "Look, if you don't want to go--" He shrugged. "It's fine. I thought you'd like it. Maybe I was wrong."

Abby found herself smiling, despite her reservations. "I *would* like it," she said. "But it's probably not a good idea. I don't have anything to wear. And I've been driving home every night; I don't have anywhere to stay, either."

"Oh, you could stay at the teahouse," Seth said, dismissing that problem with a wave of his hand. "There are always extra rooms, and they're fairly reasonable. At least on masquerade night, they're reasonable."

"I don't have anything to wear," Abby said, torn. "Just regular Faire garb, nothing fancy--"

"If you let me watch your booth tomorrow morning, Carmen can find you something to wear," Seth said, looking hopeful.

Abby couldn't think of any other protest. "Okay," she said. "If you really want me to go with you--"

Seth smiled. "I do," he told her.

"Okay," Abby said, suddenly shy. And then, worried, "I can't dance. I don't know any of the dances--"

"It's okay," Seth said. "I don't know them very well, and I dance about as well as you could expect someone to fake it."

"Then--then I'll see you tomorrow morning," Abby said, and couldn't help but feel a bit more optimistic about the rest of her time at the Faire.

She got into her car, waved to Seth, and drove away.

Chapter 3

The next morning, Abby pulled into the parking lot to find Seth waiting for her.

"I've been instructed to help you set up your booth," he said. "And to tell you that Carmen will be waiting at our trailer to find you something to wear." He paused. "If you still want to go."

Abby smiled. "I still want to go, yes," she said.

"And I can watch your booth while you're with Carmen, if that's okay," Seth finished, smiling now, and Abby thought he looked a bit relieved. Had he thought she would chicken out? Maybe he wasn't used to asking anyone to masquerades. Maybe he thought she would have second thoughts.

"Of course that's okay," she said. "Why wouldn't it be okay? You've watched my booth before--" She'd brought a bin of fiber with her today, along with a few drop spindles. An overnight bag; a change of garb for tomorrow; breakfast and tea, although if she was staying at the teahouse, bringing tea seemed a bit much. It was nearly twice as much as she'd packed in her car the night before.

"I just--" Seth had automatically taken the cart's handle; now, he stopped. "I'm not at all used to this," he said. "You were right. Carmen made me do it.

She said if I didn't ask you, she would ask you for me. And I couldn't let her do that."

"Well, I'm glad you asked," Abby said, and meant it, because he *was* cute, after all, and he was obviously a nice guy. "And I really appreciate your help. *All* of you, really! You've all been so nice."

"Well, when we started setting up at the Faires, we didn't know what we were doing, either," Seth said. "And it's hard to be alone, especially at something like this."

They started walking again. Abby remembered talking herself out of coming time and time again, just because she had no partner; no helper, and then her Aunt Rose had finally told her to set up anyway. 'What's the worst that can happen?' she'd asked. 'You set up, you sell a few spindles, you make some new friends. And maybe next year it won't be so hard.'

And she had, of course, been completely correct.

"It took me a long time to convince myself I should set up," she said. "I'm still not sure it was a good idea--"

"Your stuff is new," Seth protested. "Unusual, which is good. No one else is selling it. It will catch on. Faire's only been on for two weeks, after all. You have plenty of time."

He helped her set up the tent and the tables and the racks and displays of spindles. Next door, Matt did the same with Carmen's scarves, and they fluttered in a small breeze that played around the tent flaps.

When she lifted the rack of phangs into place, he stopped sorting through the bead spindles, glanced at her sharply, and asked, "What are those?"

"They're called 'phangs'," Abby said. "A rather simple type of supported spindle. It's an ancient design."

"They--" Seth hesitated, then shook his head. "They're not what I expected," he finally said. "Are you *sure* they're only used for spinning?"

"What else could you use them for?" Abby asked, confused. "As far as I know--"

"Nevermind," Seth said, but he did not look happy. "Have you sold any of them?"

"Two, yesterday," Abby said. "To a guy dressed like a pirate. Really, though, I'm not sure why he bought them. I don't think he intended to spin with them at all." She paused, trying to find the right words for what she wanted to say. "Is there something wrong? Did I--"

"No," Seth said, too quickly. "There's nothing wrong. Forget I brought it up. Please?"

"Okay," Abby said uncertainly, and he tried to smile.

"You should probably go and meet Carmen now, unless I've screwed everything up--"

"No," Abby said. "You haven't. Not yet, at least." She looked at the display of phangs, then made a decision. "You know what? I really didn't like the look of that pirate yesterday. How about we put these aside, and if he comes back, just tell him they've all sold. Okay?"

The relief on Seth's face told her she was on the right track, but she had no idea why he was so upset about their shapes. Unless-- "I wouldn't want anyone to use one as a weapon."

"A weapon," Seth latched upon that explanation as if she'd thrown him a lifesaver. "Yes. That's what they look like to me. Weapons." He flushed, then, and glanced at her sidelong. "I'm sorry. You did a great job making them."

"Thank you," Abby said, and lifted the display of phangs. "Let's set these aside anyway, okay?"

He seemed a bit relieved to have them behind the table she used as a counter, although in truth, she knew she couldn't keep them aside forever.

Her demonstration spindle was a phang, after all, and she hadn't brought any others.

She would deal with that once she returned from finding something to wear to the masquerade. Until then, they could sit behind the counter.

Even an hour before the Faire opened, it bustled with activity. She said goodbye to Seth, waved to Matt, whose smile seemed a bit too knowing, and walked back down the path to the campground with a written map of the way to their trailer, which was evidently at the back.

At this time of the morning, the campgrounds were nearly empty; she met no one on her way, although she saw a tall pirate slip into the woods near her destination, his tricorn hat tipped back at an angle, his coat blending in with the autumn-hued trees.

And she had to admit she was a bit curious to see the camper they all lived in, because she knew they traveled to the different Faires across the United States; they weren't local and they weren't part-timers. Abby couldn't imagine four people living full time in some of the trailers she passed. And perhaps theirs was a bit larger than the others, but not by much. It wasn't big enough to warrant its own motor; it sat under a tree next to a rather rusty pickup truck with a cap on the back.

A hammock hung between the tree and the camper, and a sunshade with walls created an outdoor room complete with a battered couch and a patio set that held the remains of someone's breakfast, including tea.

Carmen wasn't waiting for her, but Abby heard low voices from inside as she approached. She hesitated at the edge of the sunshade, wondering if she should step inside or hail the camper from outside its boundaries; in the end, she walked inside because Carmen was, after all, expecting her.

"But are you sure it's *safe*?" That was Carmen's voice, sounding worried.

"Of course not," came the reply. Abby did not recognize *this* voice; perhaps this was the juggler. Had Seth said his name? "I think he'll try something tonight. It's what *I'd* do, if I were him. But he'll also know I'll be on my guard tonight. So perhaps he'll wait until all the festivities are over." He paused. "It might not be safe, but we need the money to fix the truck. Abby's here."

She had just raised her hand to knock. When Carmen appeared at the door, she lowered it, smiled uncertainly, and stepped back as she opened the screen door wide.

"Come in, come in!" she said, but something in her cheery smile seemed off; she seemed worried about something. Like Seth had been worried about something. "Don't mind the mess; we're in the middle of a project, and we don't have a lot of room to spread out."

The 'mess' consisted of a small pile of paper on the only table in the camper. There was a bench and one chair; the bench was occupied by a boy--a young man, truly--with sandy brown hair and dark eyes. He was dressed in mundane clothes; a t-shirt and jeans, and looked to be about seventeen.

"Abby, this is Colin," Carmen said. "Colin; Abby."

"Seth's date," Colin said, and smiled. "You spin yarn, and make spindles. Right?"

"That's right," Abby said. "Are you the juggler, then?" She looked around the tiny space, wondering where they kept all of their supplies; their garb. How did Carmen paint her scarves when there was barely enough room for one person to comfortably stand in what passed for a kitchen?

And then, she realized that most of what she saw was storage. The chair wasn't just a chair; its seat lifted up, and so, she presumed, did the bench.

There were drawers under the bed, and cabinets and closets everywhere she looked.

"Yes," Colin said, amused by her regard. "I'm the juggler."

"The headline act during the masquerade," Abby said, because she'd pulled out a flyer once she'd made it home the night before. "You juggle knives?"

"Razor sharp knives," Colin said, and pulled a stack of paper closer. "Blindfolded." He glanced at Carmen, considering. "Although I'm not sure if I'll go with the blindfold tonight."

Abby knew they were all worried about something, but she didn't feel she knew them well enough to ask. She followed Carmen to the back of the camper--which wasn't that far away from where Colin sat--past the tiny bathroom, complete with a shower, and to a closet nearly bursting with garb.

With practiced ease, Carmen pulled out a couple of dresses and hung them on the back of the door. "I want you to pick," she said. "I think the blue one would go best with what Seth's intending to wear--"

"He likes dark colors," Colin offered from his seat at the table.

"But I really think the green and gold one--" Carmen held it up.

It wasn't a complicated dress. A long-sleeved velvet underdress in dark green with an overdress in golds and purples that looked to be hand-embroidered. The blue one was equally gorgeous; navy blue sewn with tiny silver stars.

"They don't really adhere to period rules as much at the masquerade," Colin said. "Fantasy rules, perhaps, more than anything."

"You'll see a lot of costumes," Carmen said. "Even though it's not Halloween."

"It's close enough," Colin said. He'd abandoned the papers for a small wooden box that presumably held his knives, because he'd started polishing them, even though Abby couldn't see a smudge on their shiny surfaces. "I think you should pick the blue one." He glanced up at them. "Although the green and gold go better with the color of your hair."

"I agree with Colin," Carmen said. "But what do *you* think?"

"They're both fabulous," Abby said. She held up the green and gold dress and regarded herself in the mirror on the back of the door. Colin was right; it complemented her hair and her coloring, but the blue one made her look almost--exotic. "What are *you* wearing?" she asked Carmen.

"I'm not going to the masquerade as a guest," Carmen said. "I'll be there as Colin's assistant." She said this almost as if she expected Colin to protest.

"I," he said, "have never used an assistant."

"Maybe it's time you start," Carmen said. She turned away from him, but not before he frowned at her, clearly not wanting to discuss anything in Abby's presence.

"The blue dress," Abby said to allay some of the tension.

Colin smiled. "Good choice." To Carmen, he said, "I wouldn't know what to *do* with an assistant."

"All I'd have to do is stand there and hand you things," Carmen said, and Abby saw worry--and fear--in her gaze now, although she tried her best to hide it.

Colin's face changed subtly, as if he'd sensed her fear. "I'll--consider it," he said.

Carmen's smile was quick and fleeting. "Thank you," she said, and held up the blue dress. "I think you'll look lovely."

Abby smiled. "I'll take good care of it," she promised. "Thank you so much!"

Carmen placed the dress in a zippered bag and handed it to Abby. "You're very welcome." She hesitated. "Seth's a bit shy at first. But he's a really good person."

"I thought you were all--" Abby said, then stumbled to a stop, embarrassed anew. "*Together.*"

Carmen's eyebrows rose. "We're family," she said simply. "Chosen family. He's up for grabs, if you're interested."

Abby knew her face had to be beet red. "I never would have asked," she muttered, and tried to hide behind the dress, certain Colin had to be laughing at her. But when she risked a glance at him, she saw that he'd left the table, carrying the box of knives into the tiny kitchen. And when he turned to look at her, she saw nothing pitying in his gaze.

"Do you need anything before I leave?" Carmen asked, then added, "Oh! I forgot. Abby, do you have shoes?"

"I brought a pair of flats," Abby said. "They're black--will they be okay?"

"They'll be fine," Carmen said. "Good. You're all ready then--"

"You'll need a mask," Colin said, interrupting her.

"Oh, that's right," Abby said.

"I think Grey and Toby could help with that," Carmen said. "You should ask them. They might be willing to loan you something, or trade."

"I'm not sure I have anything they'd want to trade," Abby ventured, but Colin said, "Grey uses silk in some of her work. Silk thread, mostly, but really thin handspun yarn would probably be perfect."

"Oh," Abby said, because she hadn't really thought that anyone would actually want the yarn she spun at all. "I'll ask. Thank you."

Colin smiled. "I hope you like the show," he said.

"Don't you get nervous?" Abby asked. "I can't imagine standing up in front of all those people--"

"I don't get nervous about standing up in front of all those people," Colin said. "I've been juggling in front of an audience for a very long time." He looked rather surprised she'd even asked, as if he'd never actually considered being nervous before in his life.

Abby almost asked how old he was, because he truly didn't look old enough to have been juggling in front of an audience for a handful of years, much less a very long time. "I hope everything goes well tonight, then. I'm looking forward to the show. *And* the masquerade."

"So is Seth," Colin said. To Carmen, he added, "No, I'm fine. I think I'll rest a bit before tonight." And he carried his box of knives into what passed as a bedroom in the camper, drew a curtain across the doorway, and left them alone.

"I'll walk back with you," Carmen said, and made sure the door was locked as they stepped outside.

As they walked down the path, Abby asked, "Can I ask you a question? You don't have to answer it if you don't want to."

"I think I know what you're going to ask," Carmen said. "But go ahead and ask it anyway." She sounded sad, almost, sad and worried, as if she hadn't quite decided upon her answer.

"You're all very worried about something," Abby said quietly. "Seth and Colin and you, I mean. I haven't talked to Matt today, but I'm sure he's worried too. Is it anything I can help you with? Since you've been so nice to me?"

Carmen let out a breath. "I can't tell you. It's not something I can share, not without asking the others first." She paused. "But I'll ask, okay? Because I like you, Abby, and I hope we can be friends." Her smile trembled around the edges.

"Just let me know if I can help," Abby said firmly, and dropped the subject. She didn't have any right to push, after all, or any right to know their private business. "Can you tell me how you paint your scarves? I've been wanting to get into dying fiber, but it seems so complicated."

"It's not that complicated," Carmen said, and launched into an explanation that carried them all the way back to their respective booths where Seth was, awkwardly, attempting to explain spinning on a drop spindle to a young girl and her father--early birds--and not doing that badly in his explanation at all.

He stopped when he saw Abby. "Here's the expert," he said, but the girl had already chosen her spindle, and Abby had her first sale of the day.

"You were doing pretty good there," she said, teasing, and Seth flushed. "I've been watching you spin," he told her. "It's--fascinating."

"Then maybe you should practice a bit more," Abby said. "Do you have a spindle?"

"I--ah--made one," Seth said. "But it's not as nice as yours. And Carmen had some wool she bought for a project, so I liberated it from a craft box." He hesitated. "I could show you it, if you promise not to laugh."

"I would never laugh," Abby said, and meant it.

He stepped outside, and to Carmen's tent, returning only a moment later with a small zippered bag in his hand. When he opened it and pulled out his spindle, she didn't laugh, because it wasn't funny at all. It was--perfect.

He'd cut a circle from a tree branch, drilled a hole in the middle, and sanded it down smooth. Attached a wooden knitting needle, and he had a perfectly functionally rustic spindle, and he'd left a little bark on the edges, which was absolutely *perfect*. "How does it spin?" Abby asked.

"Not that bad," Seth said, and showed her, using one of her supported spindle bowls. "I've just been using a little teacup, but it seems to work okay."

"Most of my spindle bowls--at home, at least--were picked up at yard sales," Abby admitted. "And thrift shops. And sometimes I just raid a cupboard." She picked up his spindle. "You did a great job. You could sell these, if you wanted to."

"I wouldn't encroach on your business," Seth said, almost automatically, as if he'd had this conversation before, with someone else.

"So you've made more of them?" Abby asked.

"Six more," Seth admitted. "But really, I wouldn't--" he paused. "They're kind of addicting to make. Although I'm running low on knitting needles now that I've used all of Carmen's wooden ones."

"You could bring them over here," Abby said. "If you want to sell them. I don't mind. I really like them!"

Seth looked at her carefully. "You really do?"

"I really do," Abby said. "I'm not just saying that to be polite. They're neat. Different. And I like the bark. Can I buy one? Or maybe we can do a trade?"

Seth's smile started slowly, until it spread across his entire face. The worry still lurked in the back of his gaze, but it wasn't nearly as prevalent as before. "A trade," he said. "I wouldn't know what to charge, anyway."

"Speaking of a trade," a voice said from the back of Abby's tent, "I hear you're going to the masquerade." Grey poked her head through the divider between their tents and smiled at them both.

Grey was dressed--today, at least--in a patchwork skirt and a many-pocketed vest that she used to keep her various tools and bits of stuff of the maskmaker's trade. Abby had never seen her without ribbons in her hair.

"Seth invited me," Abby said. "Carmen loaned me a dress--"

"And now you need a mask," Grey finished.

"Now I need a mask," Abby said. "And Colin mentioned you might be willing to do a trade, or a partial trade--" She'd seen the prices on Grey and Toby's masks, and knew nothing that she spun could possibly equal their cost.

Seth had picked up his spindle and put it away; he seemed almost anxious that Grey not see it, although Abby couldn't imagine why.

"I have a mask for you," Grey said to Abby. To Seth, she added, "And a message for *you* to take to Colin, if you would."

"He hasn't done anything wrong," Seth blurted out, then immediately regretted his words; Abby saw the consternation on his face before he turned away.

"No, he hasn't done anything wrong," Grey said easily, and Seth looked up at her in surprise at her tone. "Only ask him to remember that this Faire is on neutral ground. And neutral ground applies to *everyone.*" She smiled. "That's my message, and the only one I have to give. Now. Abby. Let's talk about your mask."

"I'll give him the message," Seth said. "But *everyone?* I'm sorry, but--"

"Everyone," Grey said firmly.

Seth looked rather stunned by this. "The rest of the spindles are in the camper," he finally said. "I can go get them, if you really think they might sell. And I'll pass the message along to Colin at the same time."

"Go get them," Abby told him. "We'll decide on prices, and a trade. Okay?" She had no idea what Grey meant by her words, but they sounded-- at least a little--encouraging, perhaps, in the face of whatever was worrying them.

Seth nodded and left, taking his spindle bag with him. Grey waited until she'd taken care of a--paying--customer, and then she said, "They haven't told you what they're so worried about, have they?"

"No," Abby said. "But that's okay; they barely know me. They don't have to tell me anything. I'd still go to the masquerade with Seth." She hesitated. *"You* know, though?"

"I do," Grey said. "But it's not my tale to tell. And I don't know because they told me; I know because of my position here. But that's neither here nor there, truly. All I can tell *you* is that they are in need of someone they can trust right now. All of them. And if you are a trustworthy person--which I believe you are--then continue on and they will, eventually, tell you."

Abby nodded. "Okay," she said. "I can accept that." And to her surprise, she found that her words were true. She *liked* Carmen and Matt and Seth--and Colin. "About a mask--"

"About a mask," Grey said. "What color is your dress?"

"Navy blue," Abby said. "With silver stars. Carmen and Colin said it matched what Seth was wearing, but I haven't seen what he's wearing. And I haven't asked him, either."

"Good," Grey said. "That goes with the mask I had in mind." She slipped back through the divider, then returned with a simple navy blue mask with a single silver star on each corner of the face piece. It was expertly molded out of leather, and looked to have been made specifically for Abby's borrowed dress. The tie looked to be handwoven, also out of silver, with tiny little bells on the ends.

She *almost* asked if it had been. "That's gorgeous!"

"This one you can borrow," Grey said. "For the masquerade. But this one--" and from behind her back, she produced *another* mask; a dryad mask, Abby thought. It was wooden--no, leather carved and stamped to look like wood--and tinged with greens and browns. It almost looked real. And much too costly for Abby to ever afford. "This one's a trade."

"For what?" Abby asked faintly. She couldn't tear her eyes away from the mask.

"I need a lot of handspun silk," Grey said. "In various colors."

"I could do that," Abby said immediately. "How much?"

"About half a pound," Grey said. "The colors aren't as important as the fact that it's handspun."

"Thin? Thick?"

Grey pulled a length of ribbon from one of her pockets. "Like this," she said, "Thin enough to be thread."

"I can do that," Abby said again. "I have some here with me, actually. Not enough, but I can spin more." She bent to rummage in her bag, and emerged with three small skeins of silk yarn that she had spun on one of her phangs. Silk traveled well, so she always had some silk and a spindle in her purse. And after a while, it started to add up.

"This will do nicely," Grey said. "Very nicely, in fact. Are you sure you weren't planning to use this for something?"

"I don't really use it," Abby admitted. "I've always wanted to learn to weave, but I just like to make yarn. And spindles. At least for now."

Grey smiled. "There's always time to learn something new," she said. "Thank you very much. I had hopes we could work out a trade."

"Thank *you*," Abby said. "For the trade and the mask to go with the dress."

"I hope you have fun at the masquerade," Grey said. "We'll be there too." Almost on cue, Toby called Grey's name from the other side of the divider. "See you then," Grey said, and slipped through the opening on the other side.

Maybe it was the fact that Abby had something to look forward to, or maybe it was just that when Seth came back with his spindles, he stuck around as they worked out a trade, then seemed to be satisfied to stay and help Abby at her booth instead of wandering back over to Carmen's. Neither Carmen nor Matt came over to fetch him, so Abby didn't ask why he had elected to stay with her instead of his housemates. His family.

The day passed swiftly. Abby made more sales than the day before, and Seth sold two of his spindles, something he seemed to be surprised about, although when he told Carmen, she smiled and said, "I told you so," which made him sigh and shake his head.

"Carmen's usually right," he said to Abby afterwards. "She told me I could sell them." He paused. "Actually, she told me I *should* sell them so I could buy her new knitting needles. Although I'm not sure she meant it, since she doesn't actually knit."

"I tried to knit once," Abby said. "It ended up a tangled mess. I still don't know what I did wrong. I can crochet, though, but really, I like to spin yarn more than use it for anything. And I really like to make spindles. My aunt bought me a little lathe for my birthday two years ago, and I've been making spindles ever since."

"Do you have an online shop?" Seth asked.

"Yes, but I shut it down when I set up at festivals," Abby said. "It's too complicated otherwise. Too much to keep track of, too many things to do!"

"Do you live around here?" Seth asked.

"About half an hour away," Abby said. "I rent a little cottage in Harveysburg. It's one of a thousand cute little villages in Ohio, but I like it there." She hesitated, knowing they were nomads. "What about you? Have you always traveled around?"

"I have, yes," Seth said. "My parents did, too. Colin's never done anything else, either. Carmen and Matt--they grew up in normal houses with normal families. I'm not sure--" He broke off when Carmen walked into Abby's tent.

"You're not sure what?" she asked, arching an eyebrow at him.

"Nothing," Seth said, and flushed.

"It's your turn," Carmen said. "But Matt said he'd go if you want to stay here."

It was past lunchtime by then; Abby and Seth had shared a beef stew breadbowl from one of the food vendors; Carmen and Matt had shared another of the same. No one had mentioned Colin; although there was a perfectly serviceable kitchen in the camper, it seemed odd to leave him out. But truthfully, Abby had never actually seen Colin at Carmen's booth or performing with Seth and Matt, which was strange in itself. It was almost as if he wasn't really a part of their group, even though he obviously lived with them.

"I'll go," Seth said.

Abby would have offered to go with him if she hadn't been busy with customers; she'd demonstrated--and sold--twice as many spindles as the day before, and closing wasn't for another six hours. Having someone in the booth with her made the time go quicker, and made it easier to step out if needed; she didn't have to ask someone to watch her booth for a quick trip to the bathroom or to get something to eat, or even just to step away from it all for a little while. And that was nice.

When Seth returned an hour later, he seemed subdued, but his mood improved as the afternoon wore on. Around four, Abby's booth was so packed that there was a line to get inside, and Abby saw more than one person leave Carmen's booth with one of her scarves, as well.

It was a good day. And it totally made up for the dismal sales the day before.

The Faire closed up after dark so that the people headed to the masquerade would have time to shop as well. Colin appeared right after sunset to help Carmen pack up her booth, and watching all four of them together made Abby revise her previous impression. Because although Colin seemed reticent, perhaps that was because he'd just met Abby. With the others, he seemed more relaxed; more open.

Although, they all seemed to be watching for something. And perhaps it was just because of the masquerade and Colin's performance, but Abby didn't think so.

Her room had been arranged at the teahouse; and storage for her tent and containers as well. While Seth stowed her stuff away, Abby carried her dress, overnight bags, and both masks up to her room, which overlooked the main thoroughfare.

It was a cozy room, rather plain, but comfortable enough, with a twin bed, chest of drawers, nightstand, and even a small desk. The bathroom, at least, had a shower, which Abby used to wash away the dust of the day.

Carmen arrived soon after that, and fixed Abby's hair in a complicated arrangement of curls. Abby almost didn't recognize herself in the mirror after slipping on the dress; and when she modeled it for Carmen with the borrowed mask, she felt a strange sense of unease mar the vision in the mirror. She shivered.

"You look like you stepped out of a fairy tale," Carmen said, suddenly sober, as if she'd sensed the same unease. She closed Abby's door, then turned to face her. "I talked to the others."

"And they didn't want you to tell me," Abby said easily. "That's fine; I don't mind."

"No, actually, we decided to tell you," Carmen said. "But not until after the masquerade and the show, okay? Right now, I can tell you this: there's a person at this Faire who would like nothing more than to hurt Colin. And that's why we're all on edge."

"Because Colin thinks this person will do something during his performance?" Abby asked. "Does this person have a good reason--"

"This person's reason is plausible to them, but no one else," Carmen said. "Colin hasn't hurt anyone. He hasn't broken any laws. And yes, we think he'll try something tonight. But we don't know what he actually *looks* like; he's been walking around in at least three different costumes for the past two weeks. Every time we think we've found him, he disappears." She paused. "And I think he followed us from our last Faire."

"So when Grey said this was neutral ground for everyone, she meant that Colin can't do anything to this guy?" Abby asked.

"Only in self-defense," Carmen said. "And it's not like Colin would do anything to him anyway, *except* in self-defense. But Colin didn't think the rule of neutral ground applied to him. Which is something he'll have to explain to you himself."

"Okay," Abby said. "After the masquerade and the performance. That's fine. But--should he be giving a performance?"

"I don't think so, but he disagrees," Carmen said, and smiled tightly. "Hence the reason why I'm now his assistant. We've come to a compromise. Matt's security; Seth is just going to have a nice time at the masquerade." She said this as if Seth didn't have a choice *but* to have a nice time.

"If it's too much," Abby began, but Carmen was already shaking her head, almost before Abby started to speak.

"Seth will be crushed if you back out now," she declared, although Abby wasn't quite sure that was true. "And anyway, you can keep an eye on Colin from the audience, right? We don't know if he's going to do anything tonight; it just seems like the most obvious time for him to act. And if you see anything suspicious, just tell Matt."

Seeing *anything* suspicious wouldn't be an easy task, Abby realized when Seth arrived--dressed in a vaguely Edwardian outfit, complete with a mask that was shaped as the head and partial beak of a crow, complete with feathers.

When they stepped outside the teahouse, Seth took her arm. And Abby nearly gasped in awe at the menagerie lining up outside the meadow--roped off, now, since it was a ticket-only event--and as they stepped into their place in line, she saw more fairies than she ever thought she would see in her life. Fairies, vampires, dryads--barely dressed in strategically placed leaves; tall elves straight out of the fantasy novels she'd read and reread. Everything seemed to be faintly glowing; although the buildings were dark, the path was well-lighted, although she couldn't see any streetlights at all.

They were stopped at the barrier by a person dressed like a goblin who took their tickets and directed them to a large tent for the show. Colin rated a tent, but the magician moved through the crowd and plied his trade; Abby saw him more than once; a tall, blond man dressed in multi-colored robes, his wizard's hat poking above the crowd.

Colin's tent--black and dull against the sparkling lights--seemed to be full, although Abby and Seth found seats in the middle. Abby didn't see Matt at all, although Seth didn't act as if that was unusual. The crowd inside murmured to each other in a susurrus of sound, but once a light flared up onstage, they quieted in anticipation.

Abby found she was holding her breath as a curtain swung back to reveal an empty stage, save for a large wooden box in the middle. A moment later, Colin appeared--he didn't walk out on stage; he just appeared, as if he'd been standing there all along. The crowd gasped. Colin smiled. And from then on, they were under his spell.

And it *was* a spell, Abby realized, or as close to a spell as someone could get without actual magic. Colin never spoke, but he didn't need to speak. He merely juggled, but 'merely' wasn't exactly the right word; not at all. His knives were shining streaks of silver in the air; his concentration--and his talent--complete.

It wasn't just juggling. It was an aerial ballet with razor sharp knives. When he stopped, and caught them, and bowed to the audience, the applause rang in Abby's ears. But when Carmen appeared from the side of the tent with a blindfold in her hands; and when she carefully tied it around Colin's eyes, leaving no doubt he could not see, the silence was so thick and so anticipatory that Abby wondered if she'd suddenly gone deaf.

"He never misses," Seth whispered, and it sounded like a prayer.

And Colin didn't miss. He threw the knives--a dozen of them--up in the air, and then, suddenly; somehow, they were flying in an impossible rotation that took Abby's breath away.

What was he doing at a Renaissance Festival? Hiding from someone? Despite his apparent youth, he was obviously a professional. Well-trained, even. And Seth was right. He never missed, not even when a commotion at the back of the tent caused some in the audience to look around, the spell temporarily broken.

"Matt," Seth said with satisfaction; without moving his gaze from the stage. Even though Colin had to have heard the commotion--which Abby couldn't see--he didn't stop; he didn't pause; he didn't falter.

That complete of concentration just wasn't possible, was it? Was the blindfold a trick? Did it matter? Because in the end, Colin got a standing ovation as he stood on top the wooden box and bowed to the audience. And then, just as quickly as he appeared, he vanished, leaving one silver knife stuck into the top of the box and nothing more.

Nearly every person in the audience put money into the bucket Carmen carried around. When it reached Abby, she saw twenties--and even a hundred dollar bill inside. She reached for her wallet, but Seth stayed her hand. "You don't have to," he said.

"That was--like going to the Cirque De Soleil and having first row seats!" Abby said. "I can't believe he's *that* good. It was amazing!"

Seth smiled. "He'll be happy to hear you liked his performance," he said as they rose to file out of the tent.

"What is he doing here, though?" Abby asked. The bucket had come round again; it was almost brimming with bills. Abby put in ten dollars, but she would have put in more if she'd brought more. Seth didn't comment.

"What do you mean?" Seth asked, almost too nonchalantly.

"He's--" Abby fell silent as they approached the doors, because Colin stood there with Carmen at his side, accepting compliments and praise; basking in the well-wishes of the crowd even as he watched them for any sign of deceit or betrayal. And he *was* watching; Abby saw him move away from a woman dressed like an Egyptian Queen, but not so quickly that the woman would have noticed.

And when they approached and he recognized them, Abby saw him relax. Again, it was subtle; barely there. But she'd been watching for it, and she saw it.

And so did someone else. A flash of color out of the corner of her eye; Abby started to turn her head, but the person was already moving away, his tall wizard hat still poking above the crowd. When she looked back at Colin, she saw uncertainty in his gaze for one swift second before the mask--the performance mask; the automatic smile, slightly frayed around the edges now--returned.

Abby assumed they would join the crowd outside, but Seth seemed to want to stay by Colin, and she didn't mind, considering the look that had been on his face. After a little while, Matt returned empty-handed, but he gave Colin and Carmen and Seth a pointed look.

And then, they were alone in the tent, with the noise of the crowd outside. Someone started to play a tune--a waltz, Abby thought, a sprightly waltz that drifted through the air as if from far away, cutting through the silence only long enough for Colin to speak.

"Go have fun," he said. "Dance. Come back to the camper when you're done, and we'll talk." He looked as if he intended to slip away, or vanish, so Abby said, "That was the most awe-inspiring performance I've seen in my entire life."

"Why don't you come with us?" Carmen asked.

"It's probably not a good idea," Colin said--automatically, Abby thought.

Matt looked as if he agreed with Colin, but he held his tongue.

"You can't just come to the performance and not go to the masquerade," Colin said when no one moved.

"That's what *you're* doing," Seth said. "And there's safety in numbers, wouldn't you agree?"

Colin couldn't argue with that; Abby saw him try, and fail, to come up with a good response. He looked at each of them in turn. Sighed. "I didn't want it to be like this."

"Carmen and I will go back with you," Matt offered. "Seth and Abby can stay here."

"If you're staying because of me, remember I can't dance," Abby said quietly. "Was it the magician?"

"There's too many people here for me to track one of them," Colin said indistinctly, his eyes nearly closed. "That wasn't the magician; just someone dressed like him. The magician's still outside."

"Hiding in plain sight," Carmen said. "Clever."

"Not clever," Colin said, and opened his eyes. "Persistent. One dance for all of you, then. Even if you don't know how to dance. One dance, and then we all go back to the camper."

"Or to my room in the teahouse," Abby suggested. "If that's safer."

"I'm not sure I'd be welcomed in the teahouse," Colin said cautiously.

"That's also neutral ground," came a voice from right outside the tent flap. "May we come in?"

It was Toby, with Grey right behind him, both dressed in rather tattered finery, but wearing the fox masks that Abby had admired on the walls of their booth. Grey's was white; Toby's red.

Without speaking, Carmen, Matt, and Seth drew closer to Colin, almost protecting him, but Abby couldn't imagine what they intended to protect him from. Grey and Toby were *not* the enemies. Abby knew that without even questioning their motives.

"We enjoyed your performance," Grey said to Colin.

"Thank you," he replied. "I didn't know you were watching." He said this, then cocked his head to one side, considering both of them. "It might have been the masks, shielding you."

Toby nodded. "That's how they work," he said. "We brought you one to wear, if you'd like to stay at the masquerade a bit longer." He held out a plain white mask with no design at all, just white leather, formed into a face. "Since this is neutral ground, we can't do anything unless you are attacked. I'm sorry."

Colin nodded. "I understand." But he made no move to take the mask.

"You needn't see this as an obligation to owe us a favor," Grey said solemnly. "Merely the only thing we can do to keep you somewhat safe here."

Abby hadn't asked before, but she wondered now, about Grey's talk of their position at the Faire. They seemed to be much more than maskmakers, now.

"If we meant you harm, we wouldn't go about it like this," Toby said. "There are much simpler ways to make your life miserable."

"That's true," Colin said, and accepted the mask. Slipped it on. Glanced at the others. "How do I look?"

"Like the Phantom of the Opera," Carmen said, but she was smiling now, relieved.

"Thank you," Colin said to Grey and Toby, and for the first time, Matt relaxed a bit in his vigilant stance at Colin's side.

"I still don't know how to dance," Abby said.

"It's not hard," Grey told her. "I'll show you the steps." She glanced at Seth. "Both of you. Okay?"

"Okay," Seth said.

"Okay," Abby echoed, although she wasn't sure knowing the steps would do her any good.

Grey held out her hands. "Come with me," she said, and led them both outside.

The meadow had been transformed into a magical fairyland with twinkling lights strung in the trees and above the dancers. The band--one of the Faire bands--were in the middle of another waltz, and Grey showed them the steps as they hovered on the edge of the crowd. Once Abby realized no one was paying them any attention, she relaxed enough to remember Grey's instruction. Once Seth figured out where to put his feet, they managed to keep in time with everyone else, although they weren't quite brave enough to try a reel.

Abby saw Carmen dancing with Matt at one point, and then Carmen with Colin near the tent. She spotted the magician twice, but he seemed to be just a magician again, pulling roses out from behind ladies' ears and presenting them with a courtly bow. Nothing seemed to be amiss; nothing bad had happened; the night wore on until the band played their last tune, the dancers bowed to their partners, and everyone started to drift away.

It was after two in the morning. And they all had to set up their tents and their inventory in less than six hours. Abby knew she'd regret it later, but she wasn't at all tired yet. Despite her initial hesitation, she'd enjoyed herself.

"Where to now?" she asked, following Seth to Colin's tent. Matt stood outside the flap, which was closed.

"Carmen and Colin are inside," he said as they approached. "Carmen's gathering up the money; Colin's fetching his knives. Tomorrow is going to be hell, you know? I'm almost tempted to just stay up the rest of the night."

Carmen joined them a few minutes later, carrying a box, which Matt took from her without asking. "Someone needs to take this to the bank in the morning," she said. "I'd say tonight, but it's already morning." She yawned. "Where's Colin?"

Both Matt and Seth were suddenly on alert. "With you," Seth said. "Matt said he was with you."

Carmen shook her head. "He said he was going out. I was still counting money. But I didn't *hear* anything--I--" She turned back to the tent, her eyes wide.

Matt shoved the box towards Seth, who, in turn, handed it off to Abby. They vanished into the tent. Carmen was right behind them.

Abby entered after a moment, snagging a flashlight no one had thought to grab and turning it on. The benches still stood in place; but a group of them on the other side of the room had been pushed aside. With the money box pressed against her chest, Abby walked straight to the spot where she feared she'd find Colin, but there was only a damp, dark place on the ground, nothing more.

At first, she didn't see Carmen or Matt or Seth anywhere, but she saw a flash of white a few rows ahead, and realized what it was as soon as she approached. Colin's mask.

Abby picked it up. It seemed to be undamaged.

Seth appeared on the stage, his own mask hanging down around his neck now. "Did you--" he started, but Abby held up the mask and he fell silent, staring at it as if she'd held up Colin's severed head instead.

Carmen and Matt emerged from the back of the stage. Carmen carried the box of Colin's knives. "One's missing," she reported.

"They're silver," Matt said in a strangled voice.

A knife was a knife, as far as Abby was concerned. "Something happened back here," she said, and showed them the disturbed benches. "And I found the mask up here. But I don't see Colin anywhere."

And then she turned around, and swept the light across the ground and the shadows between the benches leaped out of its way. Until she reached a bench not far from the door and saw a darker shadow amid the others; an outstretched hand pale in the wash of her light; Colin's face, hidden under a bench that had toppled--or had *been* toppled--over his outstretched form.

Abby dropped the box of money. It was either that or the flashlight, and she thought they'd need the flashlight, since she saw blood on Colin's shirt. Blood, and a very familiar--*distressingly* familiar--spindle sticking grotesquely out of his back.

The bloodwood one. That the pirate had purchased the day before.

"Oh--" Abby reached forward. Hesitated, not knowing whether or not it would be worse for Colin if she pulled it out. Carmen answered the question by doing just that, and covering the wound with one of her scarves. Matt and Seth pulled the bench back up and moved it away.

Colin did not move.

"Is he--" Abby didn't know what to do. "Should I call 9-1-1?" Without a cell phone? She picked up the box of money again. Realized she was still wearing the mask, and pulled it down to hang around her neck. The bells on the ends of the ribbons chimed softly.

"Don't call anyone," Matt said quickly, and glanced up at her as if he expected her to have a cell phone in hand, dialing the numbers.

"I--I didn't bring my cell phone," Abby admitted.

"Sit down," Carmen said, not unkindly. "Please."

Abby sat. She couldn't think of anything else to do.

Carmen and Seth had a whispered conference; Matt roamed the aisles, presumably checking to make sure the man who had attacked Colin wasn't hiding beneath the benches. Abby kept the light trained on Colin's motionless form. When he moved, she was certain she'd moved the light instead, and that *her* movement had given him the illusion of life. But then he raised his head and tried to get up. And Carmen and Seth hurried to help him.

"I'll be f-fine," he whispered, but he didn't look fine; he looked covered in blood and bleeding from more than one wound. He slumped against the bench, his face almost as pale as the moon outside. When he saw Abby, he tried to straighten up, as if to pretend in her presence was much more important than admitting that fiction to anyone else.

"I can find a phone and call an ambulance," Abby ventured, somehow knowing Colin would refuse.

He closed his eyes. "I don't need an ambulance," he whispered.

"The camper won't be safe," Seth said softly.

"Then bring him to my room in the teahouse," Abby told them.

Colin's eyes were still closed, or else Abby thought he wouldn't have protested *that* idea, too.

Carmen hesitated. "Will you hand me his mask?" she asked. "It seemed to work, before; we could sneak him in--"

"Not a good idea," Matt said, but didn't elaborate.

Carmen sighed. "No, you're right. Not a good idea. Will you and Seth carry him? Abby and I will clear the way. Give us a few minutes lead."

Seth and Matt took up guard positions beside Colin. Abby followed Carmen outside, which was now deserted. Any cleanup would happen after dawn.

"Does this have something to do with why you were all so worried?" she asked.

"Yes," Carmen said, moving quickly through the quiet streets. Abby almost had to run to keep up with her. "But let's get him somewhere safe first, okay?" She sounded like she was crying now, or trying to hold back tears.

They arrived at the front door of the teahouse. Carmen knocked, but the door swung open under her fist. The common room was dark and quite deserted, but Abby heard noises back in the kitchen, and that's where they found the proprietress drinking tea, of course, still dressed in her gown from the masquerade, her own mask abandoned on the table.

Her name was Margaret, but everyone called her Meg. *Madame* Meg, truthfully, which went with the name of the teashop--Madame Meg's Marvelous Mixes.

"My dears," she said, and climbed to her feet. "You look completely exhausted." She raised an eyebrow. "And you're going to be even *more* exhausted tomorrow--"

"Colin was attacked after the masquerade ended," Carmen said. Perhaps she'd meant to break the news gently; perhaps she'd decided that the bald truth would be better, since they'd told Matt and Seth to give them a few minutes, not half an hour. She took a deep breath. "We need to bring him somewhere safe."

"This is the safest place in the entire Faire," Madame Meg said, serious now. "Bring him here. I'll swear on anything you like that he will not be harmed."

Carmen nodded, her eyes bright with tears. "Thank you," she managed to say before she met Matt and Seth at the door. They carried Colin between them, as if he'd drunk too much at the masquerade, but he was still unconscious. His head lolled against Seth's shoulder; the mask hiding his features only causing to accentuate the fact that he was unable to protect himself. Unable to fight back if someone were to attack him again.

His skin was as pale as the mask now. The blood almost glowed against it.

Madame Meg took one look at him and her lips pressed into a thin line. "Follow me," she said; almost ordered, and led the way up the stairs. She opened the door next to Abby's room, shut both the shutters and pulled the curtain over the only window, and motioned towards the bed. "There's a connecting door between Abby's room and this one. I suggest you use it. No one will enter this building who wishes him harm. What do you need me to do before dawn?"

Before dawn seemed important, but Abby couldn't imagine why. Dawn was right around the corner, after all, and her head now swam with traitorous weariness. She watched as Madame Meg opened the connecting door; watched as Seth and Matt gently lowered Colin to the bed and removed the white mask.

Colin's eyelids fluttered, but he didn't wake up.

"Maybe a few pillows?" Carmen asked. "We can take care of--the other." She winced at the sight of Colin's chest when Seth unbuttoned his shirt. "Bandages?" And then, belatedly, "Thank you."

"That's what we're here for," Madame Meg said, and bustled off to gather up supplies.

"Can I help?" Abby asked, still not sure why they hadn't called an ambulance; still not sure what the secret was about Colin, or why he'd been attacked. Madame Meg had left them blankets, pillows, and bandages; Carmen and Matt were taking turns sponging the blood from Colin's wounds, which seemed to have stopped bleeding.

Anguished, Carmen said, "I know we said we'd talk to you about all of this after the masquerade. But can it wait until morning?" She turned to look at Abby. "Please?"

Abby stood up. Swayed. "Of course," she said, and left them alone with Colin. Walked into her room. Barely got out of her dress and into pajamas before falling forward on the bed, and into sleep.

Chapter 4

At dawn, someone started singing outside her bedroom window. Abby cracked open her eyes, realized that at some point someone had closed the connecting door, and tried to decide the merits of attempting to go back to sleep for an hour or two, or venturing into the other room to see if Colin had lived through the night. The fact that Carmen slept on the floor of her room was a promising development, because she couldn't imagine any of them actually sleeping if Colin had taken a turn for the worse.

She slipped out of bed. Tiptoed to the door, and eased it open. The other room was encased in darkness; not even a sliver of light seeped past the shutters or the curtains. But there was enough light from her doorway to allow her to see that Colin still lay in the bed, and two dark forms on the floor--amid blankets and pillows--were presumably Matt and Seth.

"I'm not dead," Colin whispered. "If that's what you were wondering."

"It was," Abby said, her voice equally soft. "And I'm glad you're not dead."

"There's something I need to tell you," Colin said. "But I want to give you the option of refusing to know, first."

"I don't think I have that option anymore," Abby said. "The spindle he used to stab you--I made that. It's called a phang. It's an ancient design. And I never meant--" She was miserable, suddenly, that something she had made had caused this.

"Not your fault," Carmen said from behind her. She yawned, moved past Abby into the darkness. "Colin, I'm turning on the light."

"I thought you made spindles to spin yarn," Colin said, squinting in the sudden brightness. He looked--marginally--better, although Abby supposed that just the fact he was awake was an improvement from last night.

"Apparently, one was used as a weapon," Abby said. "A pirate bought two of them yesterday. Bloodwood, and Walnut. He used the bloodwood one on you."

Colin made a strangled noise that sounded like he was trying not to laugh. Carmen glared at him. "It's not funny," she snapped.

"It *is*," Colin insisted. "Or, it would be if it didn't hurt so much. Will you--" He motioned towards the window.

"Why can't you just say it?" Carmen asked.

"Proof," Colin said simply, and then, to Abby, "You might want to sit down for this."

Abby sat. Matt and Seth slept on, undisturbed by the light or the activity. At her look, Carmen said, "They can sleep through almost anything," and opened the window.

She found a safety pin in a drawer. Pricked Colin's finger with it, then wiped the blood on a tissue. Placed the tissue on the windowsill, where it promptly burst into flames and burned into ash before Abby's startled gaze.

"If I put my hand on the windowsill, it would burn, too," Colin said. "And if I stepped outside--"

"I don't understand," Abby whispered. "How is that possible?"

"I was born in 1903," Colin said. "When I told you I had been standing up in front of audiences for a very long time, I wasn't joking."

He sounded so rational; so--calm.

"But--but you look younger than me!" Abby protested. She'd raised her voice; for the first time, Seth stirred. Matt slept on. "How is that possible?"

"The word you're looking for is 'vampire'," Colin said.

"The *myth*, you mean?" Abby stammered. "Because I'm pretty sure vampires don't actually exist."

"Tell the Hunter who tried to kill me that," Colin said. "And see what he says."

Abby opened her mouth. Closed it again. Glanced at Carmen, who waited patiently for her acceptance. Carmen had never seemed to be crazy. Neither had Seth or Matt.

And she remembered thinking that Colin must have been practicing for years to get that good. That he should have been in the professional circuits, not a lowly RenFaire. How he'd just *appeared* on stage, and vanished again after his performance. How she'd never seen him at Carmen's booth before dark. How--

"Oh," she said. "Oh, I see." And then, because she had to ask, "What else? If vampires are real, then what else is real?"

"Maybe you should just stick with vampires for a little while," Carmen said kindly.

"*You're* not--" Abby began.

"We're human," Seth said from where he now sat on the floor. He nudged Matt with his foot. "Wake up. It's past dawn."

Matt groaned and pulled his pillow over his head. And then, muffled, he asked, "Colin?"

"I'm awake," Colin said. "And reasonably intact."

Matt raised his head. "Do you need--" He saw Abby then, and stopped.

With a shock, she realized that they weren't just Colin's traveling companions and chosen family. They were his source of food, as well. Because vampires drank blood. Human blood, at least if those legends were correct.

"So the Hunters probably think you have them under some sort of spell," Abby heard herself say. "And that you're some evil creature preying on the innocent."

"That sounds about right," Colin said. "How can I prove to you that I am not?"

"I think you already have," Abby said, remembering his actions inside the tent after he'd been stabbed. She also remembered what Matt had said about his knives. "Wait--your knives are silver?"

"Yes," Colin said, and before he could ask, Carmen told him, "We haven't found the missing one yet, but I'm sure it will turn up."

"Silver as in werewolves can be killed by a silver bullet?" Abby asked.

"Yes," Colin said.

"Does that apply to vampires, too?" Abby tucked the knowledge about werewolves away. Since Colin hadn't denied they existed, she had to suppose that they did.

"Yes," Colin said again.

"And you--juggle them?" Abby asked, aghast. "What if you *missed?*"

"He never misses," Seth said, as he'd said before, during Colin's performance the night before.

"But what if you did?" Abby pressed.

Colin stared at her. "Where is the challenge, otherwise?" he asked. "If I miss, then I die. So I never miss."

Carmen closed the window and pulled the curtains over the shutters. The tension had drained from her shoulders; apparently, she'd expected Abby to take the news that Colin was a vampire differently. Or badly. But Abby found herself strangely accepting.

She supposed she could have gone down the path of the Hunters and believed that Colin had placed some sort of spell on all of them, but Grey obviously knew what Colin was, and also Toby. And Madame Meg as well. And they hadn't been alarmed or disgusted or armed with wooden stakes.

And why *shouldn't* Colin drink from his companions? It was probably much safer to do that than accost some stranger for his dinner. And neither Carmen, Matt, nor Seth looked any worse for wear.

"What now?" she asked.

"What now what?" Matt was still half asleep. He yawned.

"Do we set up our booths today? Go about our normal business? Try to find the vampire hunter and--" do what? Chase him away? Abby suspected he would just come back. "What are you planning to do to him?"

"This is neutral ground," Colin said. "*He* attacked *me*. I believe that allows a bit of leeway for retaliation so that he won't be able to do it again."

"And that means what?" Abby asked. "Killing him?" She felt she had to say it, because well, because Colin *was* a vampire, after all.

"I don't just go around killing people who want me dead," Colin said patiently.

"That's good," Abby said, but that still didn't explain what he--or they, she supposed--intended to do.

"But I think this Hunter has followed us from another Faire," Colin said. "And so does Carmen. And if he's following *us*, not just *me*, that means I can't do what I would usually do to avoid him."

"And what's that?" Abby asked.

Colin hesitated. "Disappear. I've--I've never been with a group of people for so long. I think that's part of the reason why the Hunter has found me."

"We haven't told anyone," Seth said.

"Not a soul," Matt echoed.

Carmen seemed to feel she didn't have to deny anything; she only looked at Colin steadily, waiting for him to continue.

"I'm more visible now," Colin whispered. "More people know what I am than ever before. I used to be able to hide from the Hunters. Now--"

"You are *not* leaving us," Carmen said.

"What if it's too dangerous for you if I stay?" Colin cried, both frustrated and angry, not that he could do much about it, lying in bed. He took a deep breath. Let it out. Closed his eyes. "If something happened to you because of me--"

Someone knocked on the door. With a dreadfully horrible look on his face, Colin opened his eyes.

"I've brought tea," Madame Meg said from the other side of the door, and everyone except for Colin relaxed.

Abby let her in. She'd brought not only tea, but breakfast, too, scones and biscuits with ham and cheese. Victor, her second-in-command, carried in a small table and a couple of folding chairs.

"Have a picnic," he said. "An inside picnic. Eat breakfast. Drink tea. The Faire's opening an hour later this morning, so you have time."

"Thank you," Carmen said, taking charge of the tray. "And thank you for giving us a room last night. What do we owe you?"

"Goodwill," Madame Meg said promptly. "And one promise."

Colin had closed his eyes again, but at this, he opened them. "What promise?"

Madame Meg waited until Victor had left before she replied. "That you not flee for your life," she said. "That you stay with your friends. That you fight for the life you've made with them. Because unless I'm wrong, they would fight for *you*."

"I don't want to leave," Colin said.

"Then don't," Madame Meg replied.

"But what if I've made them a target?" This seemed to be the crux of Colin's argument; the fact that he'd put them all in danger, however fleeting. Would a Hunter truly go after humans instead of a vampire? Abby didn't know enough about Hunters to answer that question.

"You've done nothing wrong," Madame Meg said. "Unless there's something we don't know."

For some reason, Abby thought 'we' should have been capitalized in that sentence. Because Madame Meg wasn't just talking about herself and Victor; she'd included someone else in that assumption of Colin's innocence, too, although Abby couldn't imagine who. Grey and Toby? Perhaps.

"There's nothing that would warrant a death sentence from a Hunter," Colin said after a moment. "Other than the fact that I exist."

"And that's just not good enough anymore," Madame Meg said simply. "Will you allow us to help?"

"I don't want anyone to die because of me," Colin said.

"I know," Madame Meg told him. "But sometimes that's not possible. Will you allow us to help?"

Colin looked at his friends; his chosen family. His gaze lingered longest on Abby, however. "Do you wish we hadn't told you?" he asked.

"I'd be mad if you hadn't," Abby said. "How long will it take you to recover?" She was already thinking about the week ahead.

"We usually park the camper in the park's campground for the week," Carmen said. "And travel into town to do laundry and shop for groceries."

"That might not be the best idea for this week," Madame Meg said gently.

"If you're going to suggest we leave him somewhere, forget it," Matt said.

"How long will it take for you to recover?" Abby asked again, then realized why Colin had not answered her before. "Is this the first time this has happened to you?"

"Every other time, I've been gone before the Hunters could act," he whispered, and shifted a bit in his bed. "Except this time." He lifted his arm; touched his chest. Abby saw bandages under his shirt. "It hurts."

"I'm sorry," Abby said, guilty anew. To Madame Meg, she added, "The Hunter used a spindle I made to stab Colin."

"It's still not your fault," Carmen said. "He could have used a tree branch and it would have worked just as well."

"I don't know," Colin said, finally responding to her question. "A day or so? I think I lost a lot of blood."

"There was quite the grass fire this morning when they took down your tent," Madame Meg commented. "Oh, and we found this." She produced Colin's missing knife and set it on the table amid the breakfast dishes. "Why don't you all eat. And I will go catch up on gossip. And then we can reconvene later and decide where you'll stay this week."

"You can stay at my house," Abby said, "but there's not a lot of room. I doubt that would be a problem, though, and I have a washer and dryer, so you wouldn't have to go to the laundromat." She frowned. "Although there's a lot of wood and spindles in my house--"

"I'd say we wouldn't want to impose, but that would be silly," Carmen said. "Are you sure?" She glanced at Madame Meg. "Would it be safe?"

"A house would be safer than a camper," Madame Meg said. "And if Colin wears that mask when you leave--in fact, if you *all* wear your masks--I think we can arrange it so the Hunter doesn't follow. But he'll know you'll come back. And he'll be waiting for you."

The Faire opened again on Thursday. That gave Colin three days to recover. From what he looked like now, Abby doubted he would be recovered enough to combat the Hunter by Thursday, unless the blood Carmen, Matt, and Seth intended to donate would do the trick. Weren't vampires supposed to recover quickly from any wound? Or was that more fiction than fact?

"I know," Colin said. "And he won't stop until I'm dead. I know you mean well, but I'm not--"

"Colin," Carmen said, a warning in her voice.

Colin closed his eyes. After a moment, Madame Meg tiptoed out and left them alone.

Colin's eyes were closed throughout breakfast, although Abby wondered if he were truly asleep.

When he finally opened his eyes, Carmen said, "I hope you realize that if you ever want to leave, you're free to go. But not like this, okay? Not like this." She glared at them all. "And that goes for anyone in this room."

"I'm not going anywhere," Matt said.

"I don't have anywhere else to go," Seth said, munching on a scone.

"You can't kick me out right after letting me in," Abby informed them all, but especially Colin.

"Maybe after I feel better, things will look differently," Colin finally said. "I won't leave you." He took a deep breath. "I promise I won't leave you."

"Then we won't leave *you*, either," Carmen said.

Colin nodded. His eyes slipped shut again. Abby realized that they were dancing around what needed to be done, and stood. "I'm going to go get ready for setup," she said. "If we're still setting up today."

"I think we should," Carmen said after a moment.

"We don't have any performances scheduled today, so Matt or I will help you with your tent," Seth said, but Abby knew that it would be Seth helping her, not Matt. At least, if Seth could help it.

She nodded. "Thank you." And then she left them alone with Colin, and went to pack up her things.

Chapter 5

Madame Meg had not insisted that Abby remove all her things, so she left the dress behind for Carmen and packed the rest of her things. Setting up her booth after what had happened seemed almost silly, but then again, doing something totally mundane helped allay the worry and fear for Colin's safety.

Once Seth had helped her set up her tent and arrange everything to her liking, he did the same with Carmen, since Matt had volunteered to be the first one to stay with Colin.

They intended to switch off as the day progressed, and Abby had insisted that she be put on the rotation. It was only fair, after all, and, provided Colin felt up to talking, she had a list of questions she wanted to ask him.

Although most of her questions seemed needlessly prying, at least to her mind.

When she returned the star mask to Grey and Toby, she knew without a doubt that Madame Meg had meant Grey and Toby--and perhaps even others--when she'd said 'we' that morning. Because they both knew what had happened even before she stepped through the divide.

"How is he?" Grey asked, concern clear on her face.

"Hurting," Abby said. "This never should have happened."

"Neutral ground is true neutrality," Toby said quietly. "If we had acted to keep the Hunter away from the Faire, then we would have broken the rules. But now that the Hunter has broken the rules--"

"What if he had *died?*" Abby asked.

"We gave him protection," Grey said. "And he took off the mask. For all we know, the Hunter intended to harm Carmen to get to Colin; everyone knows of his relationship with them. Or, everyone who knows what he is knows of their relationship."

"What would have happened if he hadn't taken off the mask?" Abby asked.

"The Hunter would not have found him," Toby said.

"And their relationship? The powers-that-be who know what Colin is approve?"

"The 'powers-that-be', as you put it, don't go around breaking up working relationships," Grey said, although she seemed amused at the description. "Carmen, Matt, Seth--and you--are all consenting adults. There seems to be no indication that Colin keeps them with him through deceit. In fact, from what I heard, *they* sought *him* out."

"It's funny how stories get around," Seth said from the other side of the divider.

Abby wondered how long he'd been there. She pulled aside the curtain, and he stepped through.

"You had a customer," he said. "Or, rather, *I* had a customer, although I tried to get them to buy one of yours instead."

"You don't have to do that," Abby told him, feeling awkward now, as if she'd somehow betrayed his trust by talking about them behind their backs.

But Seth showed no sign that he cared. "We *did* seek him out," he said to Grey and Toby. "We arranged it so he could free himself from captivity, and arranged it so he'd take shelter in our camper. And Plan B was to go in there and get him ourselves. Which we were fully prepared to do."

"That could have gone wrong on so many levels," Grey said as Abby wondered how someone could keep a vampire captive.

"But it didn't," Seth said. "And it hasn't."

"You said 'we' arranged it, but it was *you*, wasn't it?" Toby asked abruptly.

Seth glanced at Abby. She saw when he decided not to lie to them, and knew her presence had something to do with it. "Yes," he said. "I arranged it. But Carmen and Matt were more than willing to help."

Grey looked at him closely. Seth tensed, but she didn't ask any additional questions. "May I come to see him later?" she asked. "I trust he's somewhere safe?"

"He's in the teahouse," Seth said.

Grey and Toby exchanged looks. "Fort Knox!" they both said at the same time. And then, Grey added, "He's safe there. *Very* safe there."

"We're, um, staying with him throughout the day," Seth said. "We've got shifts."

"Good idea," Toby said. "And his mask? Does he still have it?"

"Yes," Seth said. "It's on the bedside table."

"If he goes *anywhere*, he needs to wear the mask," Grey told him. "And he needs not to take it off."

"He said--" Seth hesitated. "He told me this morning that the Hunter suspected he was in the tent. And that the Hunter said he would go after Carmen if Colin did not appear."

"Does Carmen know this yet?" Abby asked.

"No." Seth looked uncomfortable now. "She's not going to be happy when he tells her."

If he told her at all, Abby thought, but she didn't say that out loud.

"For what it's worth, we warned the Hunter, too," Grey said. "Not just Colin. And he chose to break the rule of neutral ground, not Colin."

"Colin said something about retaliation," Seth said. "But you're not going to let him go up against the Hunter, are you? By himself?"

"*We*," Toby said, again using that royal 'we', "Are only guardians, not the powers-that-be that Abby thinks we are. The rule of neutral ground is not of our making. The Queen decreed it so, and even Hunters need abide by it or suffer the consequences."

"And what are the consequences?" Abby asked, wondering if the Queen was the same one who walked at the head of the parade every day. She suspected Toby spoke of a different Queen, however.

"If someone breaks the rule of neutral ground--no matter the victim-- then *everyone* is threatened," Grey said quietly. "There *will* be retaliation, but that will have to be handled carefully, since this is a public venue. And we have thousands of people who think elves and fairies--and vampires--belong only in books and movies walking through here each and every day."

Elves and fairies and vampires. And werewolves, Abby remembered. The list was getting longer. "So wait," Abby said. "All of the fairy wings? The elf ears? Don't tell me--"

Toby grinned. "Not all, but most," he said. "This Faire is very close to the Veil that separates Faerie from this world. So we get a lot of travelers."

Seth looked ill, all of a sudden, as if he hadn't quite realized this.

"But it's still neutral ground," Grey said, seemingly for his benefit. "For everyone who comes here."

Abby had to help a customer, then, so she left them alone with Seth, something, she realized after selling the two teenagers matching bead spindles, that might not have been a good idea, because she'd heard Seth's voice and Grey and Toby answer, but he stopped talking as soon as she appeared again.

"It's almost my time to go sit with Colin," Abby said. "Seth, can you watch the booth while I'm gone?"

"Yes," Seth said. "Of course." He looked a little better now; apparently whatever Grey and Toby had told him had helped.

"Perhaps I'll walk with you," Grey said. "If you don't mind."

"I don't mind," Abby told her, but wondered if Colin would mind.

"We can call ahead to the teahouse to warn Colin of our arrival," Grey told her, and Seth relaxed; Abby hadn't even noticed that he'd tensed up again. "And Abby, wear your mask. I want to see if we're followed."

"Should we have worn ours?" Seth asked in alarm. "We've been in and out of the teahouse all morning--"

"Not necessarily," Grey said. "The Hunter has you in his sights already. There are only--maybe two places here at the Faire safe enough for Colin to recover without fear of a second attack. So the odds that he's watching the building are pretty high. It's not a bad thing if he knows where Colin is right now. It's a bad thing if he's following all of you around, and I want to find out if he is."

"Okay," Seth said, glancing out at the crowd. "But he's been very difficult to spot. He likes disguises."

"He also has to have a bit of talent, to do what he did last night," Toby said. "Be careful. I know you're being cautious, but be very careful, too."

Seth nodded. "We will."

When Abby and Grey set off for the teahouse, Carmen was the only one in her booth; Matt presumably with Colin again, oddly enough, since he'd taken the first shift as well. Abby had snagged her travel bag with spindle and silk fiber from behind her booth, thinking that if Colin slept through her whole shift, at least she'd get some of Grey's order completed while she sat with him.

There was a goblin troupe performing in front of the teahouse, playing instruments that were cleverly disguised to look as if they'd been made out of junk. Abby hadn't seen them before, but she thought she recognized the goblin playing the fiddle as the one taking tickets at the masquerade the night before. Grey nodded to them as they approached the teahouse's front door. The goblin with the fiddle nodded back without stopping his tune, but a little girl ran up to Grey and said, "Da wants me to tell you there's been no sign, and maybe the blackguard has fled since he knows we are on to him."

She had the cutest accent, something Abby hadn't quite been able to accomplish, despite many failed efforts.

Grey nodded. "Tell your Da thank you for the information," she said. "We saw no one following, so perhaps he *has* gone to ground. But I wouldn't relax any vigilance."

The little girl nodded and ran off. With a measured glance at the goblin troupe, who were now playing *Greensleeves,* Grey opened the teahouse door and ushered Abby inside.

"No sign, no word, no nothing," Madame Meg said as soon as she saw them. "Would you like some tea with your conversation?"

"That would be helpful," Grey said. "Thank you."

"I'll send Victor up," Madame Meg said. "He's been asleep most of the morning, according to Matt."

Asleep sounded so much better than unconscious, Abby thought as they walked up the stairs and stopped at Colin's door. Matt opened it before they could knock.

"I told him you were coming, but he fell asleep again," he said. "You might have to wait a bit before he wakes up." He stepped aside to let them through the door, then hesitated. "Do I need to stay?"

"In what capacity?" Grey asked. "I mean no harm, and I believe you know that."

"Go sit with Carmen," Abby said. "She looked like she was about to fall asleep on her feet."

Guilt washed across Matt's face. "Maybe I'll bring her some tea," he said. Victor knocked on the door, then, to deliver a tray. Grey took it, and set it on the little table; Matt followed Victor out the door with only one backwards glance.

When Colin opened his eyes, he stared at them both for a moment, then said, "I smell tea."

"I asked Madame Meg to bring us some," Grey said. "To share. And I came to see how you were feeling."

"Wretched," Colin said after a moment of silence. "To share in what capacity?"

"The Hunter broke the rule of neutral ground," Grey told him. "You did not."

"I would have if he had hurt Carmen," Colin said. He started to push himself up, but only got halfway before Abby had to help. She plumped the pillows up behind his back so he could sit up, surprised at how cold his skin felt.

Was that normal? She almost asked, but with Grey in the room, wasn't quite sure if he would answer to anything that might seem a weakness.

"Or any of the others, yes," Grey said. "That would have been justifiable. The other reason why I came is to ask you to drink something for me. Not just the tea. A herbal potion, of sorts, that will combat the poison from the stake the Hunter used."

"Oh!" Colin said. "Is that why I feel as if I've been scraped off the bottom of someone's shoe?"

Grey smiled. "An apt description, I'm sure," she said. "Yes. Your wounds should be healed by now. But the poisoning will take longer to recover from.

It might not be a good idea for you to be out of commission for that long, however. Not if the Hunter tries again, or does something else to hurt you."

Abby knew she spoke of the others, and, perhaps, herself.

"And the reason why you came with Abby and not Carmen, Seth, or Matt?" Colin asked.

"Abby trusts me more than they do," Grey said. "And I'm not sure they would have allowed you to drink anything except for their blood."

"I'll drink the tea," Colin said. "And I'll drink your potion, if you think it will help."

"I *know* it will help," Grey said. "I've used it before, with success." She poured three cups of tea, then emptied a tiny blue bottle into Colin's cup. "Drink every drop if you can. It might taste a little funny, but I swear to you it will help."

Colin showed no hesitation, but Abby could very well see Grey's point. If the others were here, they would have been far more suspicious, because what if something terrible happened? It wasn't as if they could take him to the nearest hospital, or to a doctor. But after he'd drained his cup dry, he did look a bit more aware; and less likely to fall asleep mid-sentence.

"Give it some time," Grey suggested, also finishing her tea. "You should be much better by later this afternoon."

"Thank you," Colin said, and then, belatedly, "What do I owe you for this?" For the first time since Grey's arrival, Abby saw fear in his gaze.

"Continued health," Grey decided after a moment. "If this never happens again, then I will consider any debts to be fulfilled."

"I would like this to never happen again," Colin said. "Very much so."

Grey left soon after that, and Abby poured Colin another cup of tea. "Can I ask you a question?" she asked as they drank in companionable silence.

"I'm sure you have a lot of questions," Colin said. "Ask away. If I need to rest, I'll let you know."

"The most obvious one first, then," Abby said. "You can drink tea?"

"Yes," Colin said. "That's the short answer. The long answer is yes, too, but it's not--it's more of a comfort than anything else."

"You said you were born in 1903," Abby said. "So you're one hundred and eleven years old. When were you turned into a vampire?"

"When I was sixteen," Colin said. "That's why I look so young. My family was in the circus. We were traveling performers. So I really have been juggling my entire life."

"Was that something you *wanted*?" Abby asked. "To be turned into a vampire?"

"No," Colin said, and glanced away from her, as if he couldn't bear those memories. "Absolutely not. But--but after it happened, what was I supposed to do? Kill myself?" He shrugged. "I made the best of it. And at least I had a way to support myself. But it was a long time before I could trust anyone with my secret. A very, very long time." He paused. "Vampires aren't trusted, even now. By most of the people who know we exist. I think it's because we exist on blood. And people feel threatened by that."

"And the Hunters?" Abby asked.

"The Hunters have existed since vampires have existed, I'd guess," Colin said. "I've tried to stay away from them. A solitary vampire has no allies against Hunters. Some of the families have successfully fought them off, but if you don't have family at your back--"

"But you do," Abby reminded him. "You do have family at your back."

"Yes, I do," Colin said. "But that wasn't what I meant. The families are-- enclaves of vampires and humans. Wizards, too. Some werewolves." He smiled. "Yes. They exist."

"Wizards?" Abby asked. "Like, *real* magic, wizards?"

"How do you think the masks work?" Colin asked, and she stared at the white mask on the table in sudden understanding.

"Oh," she said. "My mask too?"

"Yours too," Colin told her.

"Grey and Toby said they were guardians," Abby said. "Not wizards."

"I try to avoid the guardians, as well," Colin said. "But it's harder now. I started out in the circus, but there aren't as many circuses nowadays. And the Faires--there's a specific--and very small--network of performers and vendors, other than the local folk who only do one show. Like you. And word gets around, nowadays. Much much more than before."

"So it was going to happen sooner or later," Abby said, and at his questioning look, added, "That you caught a Hunter's interest."

"Yes," he said. "And I had been trying to figure out what to do when that happened." He shifted in place, then, and Abby realized that the shadows under his eyes were just about gone. His eyes looked brighter, too. She wondered if his skin was still as cold, and reached out her hand to touch his hand. He almost pulled away, but stopped himself just in time.

"Huh," Abby said, surprised. "You're warmer. You were freezing cold when I helped you sit up."

"I feel better," Colin said cautiously. "I think that potion might have worked. Or maybe it's still working." He took a deep breath; let it out. "It doesn't hurt as badly now."

"You look much better, too," Abby said. "Will you tell me one other thing? Will you tell me how you met them? Carmen and Seth and Matt?"

"I've never told anyone that story," Colin said. "I'm sure pieces of it are known, though; it seems keeping a secret around here is beginning to be impossible." He must have seen something on her face, because he asked, "Do you know part of it, then? Did someone tell you how we met?"

"Someone told me that they sought *you* out, not that you sought them out," Abby said, which was the truth. She didn't add the part about Seth and the others rescuing him from captivity; she didn't want to betray the fact that Seth was the one who told her about that. "But it's okay. If you don't want to tell me, that's fine. We can talk about something else. I have a lot more questions, although some of them seem kind of silly now."

"Silly in what way?" Colin asked. "And that's true, what you said. I'm not sure I want to go into detail right now, but they found *me*. I was--" He paused. "I was not in a good place at the time. I was in trouble, and needed help, but I didn't have anyone to help me."

"Silly in--oh, I'm assuming it's not true that vampires can turn into bats?" Abby asked. "And that's fine--you don't have to go into detail. I just thought--"

"They saved my life," Colin whispered, not looking at her now, but *through* her, as if he could no longer see her sitting there. "I was--" He blinked, then, and said, "No. Vampires can't turn into bats. At least, *I* can't. Some vampires can turn into wolves, though. But it's different than werewolves, apparently."

"Hmm," Abby said, trying to wrap her mind around shapeshifting vampires. "So you can't fly, either? Like in the movies?"

Colin smiled. "No. And depending on the movie, I can't walk out in daylight, *can* see my reflection in a mirror, *don't* really have to be invited into places, although it's polite to do so anyway--"

"Are you immortal?" Abby asked.

"We can be killed," Colin said. "I think the 'living forever' part could be true, but the oldest vampire I've met was born during the Revolutionary War. And the pace of modern life just isn't--" He paused. "It's hard, sometimes, to adjust. To keep up. Especially now."

"I don't think that's a vampires-only problem," Abby said, because she had a *cell*phone, not a smart phone, and no data plan.

"I think it's worse for us, though, because we've seen so much already," Colin said. "And we have to stay hidden. If everyone knew that we existed--"

"They'd know about everything else, too," Abby said. "And every*one* else."

"Yes." Colin shook his head. "I don't think it would go over well." He hesitated. "I'll tell you how we met if you want me to."

"If it brings up bad memories, then I understand if you don't want to tell me," Abby said. "I'm not going to get mad if you don't."

Colin looked at her for a moment. "I think you should know," he said. "But--But I'm a little tired right now."

"Then sleep," Abby said. "I brought a spindle and some fiber; I'll be perfectly happy sitting here and spinning for a while."

Colin closed his eyes. After a little while, when his breathing had evened out and his body had relaxed, Abby leaned back in her chair and spun the silk she had brought, content to watch over him as he slept.

Chapter 6

nd he slept the rest of Abby's shift. She'd spun almost all of the silk she'd brought by the time Carmen knocked on the door; Colin twitched at her knock, but did not awaken. And so they switched places, and Abby tucked both spindle and fiber away, and made her way down the stairs after bringing Carmen up to date.

It was now late afternoon. The crowd had thinned a bit; Abby had almost forgotten to don her mask as soon as she stepped out of the teahouse, but she'd remembered when she saw the magician--or someone like him--standing in the doorway of one of the clothing vendors' shops, clearly watching the teahouse.

Or waiting for someone inside, perhaps. Either way, as she made her way back to her tent, she felt the hairs on the back of her neck prickle to attention, as if he'd noted her departure and was now following.

But she looked back three times, and saw no one behind her.

The crowd continued to thin over the rest of the afternoon. By the time the fanfare sounded, there were only a handful of cars in the parking lot. Which, Abby thought, made it more difficult for the Hunter to maneuver, but there were still plenty of people around as she packed up her booth and the tent--with Seth's help--and then helped Carmen pack up hers, since Matt had stayed with Colin.

The plan was to reconvene to the teahouse. Grey and Toby had both said they would be there as well, and Madame Meg, of course. No one thought the Hunter would act before dark, or act at all, since he had to know they were watching.

But Hunters were not exactly predictable.

They arrived at the teahouse safely. But after they stowed everything away in a storage room and trooped up to Colin's room, they found him alone, asleep, with Matt nowhere to be seen.

And even then, no one panicked, at least at first.

"Colin, where's Matt?" Carmen asked, and Colin opened his eyes. "He wanted to help you clean up," he said. "I told him I'd be fine." He looked at Carmen in dawning horror. "He must have left at least an hour ago--"

And he had, somehow, completely disappeared.

The goblin troupe, which had played in front of the teahouse all day, had watched him leave, unmolested. He'd walked down the dirt path--the quickest way to Carmen's tent--and no one had seen him since.

Abby felt sick. They'd been laughing and joking and packing up their tents and their booths with no thought to Matt, who had, apparently, been in mortal danger.

"We'll find him," Toby said; Grey had already gone out. "Don't leave, okay? Just stay here. All of you." But his gaze was on Colin, as if he expected him to sacrifice himself just to bring Matt back.

"But I could track him," Colin said, looking miserable. "I've drunk his blood."

Toby hesitated. Seemed to actually consider the possibility of allowing Colin to join the search.

"No way," Carmen said. "Absolutely positively *no way*."

"But it's *Matt*," Colin said, and Carmen's argument dried up in her throat.

"We'll all go," Seth said. "Together. In a group. Okay?"

"Is your sword sharp?" Toby asked Seth, who shook his head. "Do you know how to use one in a fight, if necessary?"

"Yes," Seth said. "Yes, I do."

"I don't," Abby said, and Carmen echoed her words.

Toby nodded. "Hopefully it won't come to that. But I'll give you a sword, Seth. Abby and Carmen, you can help Colin."

But Colin had already climbed out of bed, still wearing his bloody clothes. He stood there in front of them, swaying slightly but upright, a determined glint in his eyes.

Carmen handed him a new shirt, then had to help him put it on. But after that, he seemed to push all thoughts of weakness away, and joined them at the door. He held his mask in his hand. "I assume you want me to wear this?"

"Yes," Toby said. "I think it would be a good idea." But he made no move to put one on himself. "If you have yours on hand, wear them," he said. "If not, we'll make do."

They were a strange, menagerie as they moved through the teahouse's silent front room and to the door. Seth was the only one, other than Toby, who didn't wear a mask.

"I know you could leave us all behind," Toby said to Colin. "But please don't. We're all concerned for Matt's safety, but we're also all just human. And we can't move as quickly as you can."

"I don't think I can move very fast right now," Colin said, looking as if he wished he'd stayed in bed. "He went this way, but you know that already." He stepped out into the night, and with Toby and Seth at his side, walked into the darkness.

Abby and Carmen were right behind them.

"No jokes about horror movies, okay?" Carmen murmured. "I feel like we're the ones who will get picked off by the mass murderer first."

Abby had been thinking the same thing. And Colin looked back at them, as if he'd heard Carmen's words, and said, "Well, at least the vampire's on your side."

And then, an arrow flew from the trees, narrowly missing Seth. They all ducked, except for Colin, who set off for the trees at a run. Seth, surprisingly, was right behind him.

"Stay here," Toby said, and shoved them both in the direction of a picnic table; Carmen spun around and set off after them, fury giving her strength.

There were no more arrows. Abby saw one of the goblins brandishing a longbow as she approached, however, and realized, to her shock, that they weren't just people in costume. They were actually goblins. Costume makeup wouldn't have held up to an actual battle, and it looked like there had been one.

Abby had not been far behind them, but she felt as if she'd missed everything.

Two of the goblins lay on the ground, both groaning. Abby recognized the fiddler as one of them, and Grey, bending over the other one. She heard noises from the trees, however; apparently the battle was not yet over.

And then she saw Matt, slumped against a tree trunk with a bandage around his head and a sling on his arm. Carmen knelt beside him. She cast a worried glance over her shoulder when Abby approached.

"They went into the trees," she said. "I told them not to go. Toby told them not to go." She was holding Matt's slack hand. "Grey said he'd be okay."

"Believe what she says, then," Abby said, and followed them before she could consider the consequences.

There were fairy lights here, amid the trees, lighting the way, although she wasn't quite sure what she would find once she reached the source of all the noise. But when the noise faded and died, and she realized she had walked too far, or, perhaps, not far enough, she heard Colin's voice clearly through the trees.

"My knives had never tasted blood," he said.

"Mine have," an unfamiliar voice replied. "Many times. And now they will taste yours."

"No," Colin said. "I don't think they will."

"Then I'll slit your friend's throat, and you can watch him die," the Hunter said, because it had to be the Hunter; Abby couldn't imagine the voice belonged to anyone else. And what friend? Seth? She stepped forward, closer to what seemed to be a clearing, ringed with light.

The Hunter, dressed in magician's robes, stood to her right, holding a knife to Seth's throat. Colin stood to her left, about eight feet away from the Hunter, two knives in each hand.

But they weren't *his* knives. They were similar in style, but not quite as shiny; not nearly as old. And Abby was willing to bet that the Hunter did not know this; that he hadn't studied Colin's knives or watched him carefully tend to them.

Toby stood behind Colin, frozen in place. Waiting for some sort of signal or sign to proceed.

"But these aren't my knives," Colin said, and moved in a blur; using up all of his remaining energy, Abby thought, in one last burst of effort to save Seth.

And Seth had also been waiting for a sign. As the first knife sank into the Hunter's forearm, causing him to drop his knife, Seth twisted away from him and fell to the ground. The second knife sliced deep into the Hunter's neck, but he caught it with his other hand; he caught it and he threw it back towards Colin, who neatly snatched it out of the air and tossed it back towards him.

This time, the knife missed, and *thunked* into the trunk of the tree right behind the Hunter, who dropped to his knees beside Seth, scrabbling for his knife, aiming, Abby thought, to finish him off.

But Colin pulled Seth away. Again, moving too fast for anyone but, perhaps, the Hunter to track, and in that instant where his attention was on Seth and not the Hunter, the Hunter calmly pulled the other spindle--walnut, Abby noted--from a pouch on his belt and lunged for Colin.

"No!" Abby shouted the word and ran forward, into the clearing. "No!"

Colin twisted away, but he was tiring now; tiring badly, and even though Toby's intention was to come to his aid, Abby knew he would be too late. The Hunter raised the spindle.

"No," Abby said, softer now, speaking to the trees; the fairy lights; the forest itself. "That's not what it was made to do. That's not how I intended for it to be used. It's not a weapon. It's a *spindle*."

And as if her words had triggered something, the Hunter--quite suddenly--could not move. Couldn't lower his hand, still upraised above Colin's prone form. Couldn't press his other hand against his throat, which was bleeding quite badly now, Abby noted. Perhaps Colin's second throw had nicked an artery. Perhaps the Hunter would, eventually, die from this. She decided that she really didn't care.

The lights had dimmed. The forest held its breath in anticipation.

"*We*," Madame Meg said, using that royal 'we' again; appearing from behind Toby as if she'd been there all along, "*We* will take over from here."

Abby helped Seth stand. He was bleeding from a small cut on his throat, but seemed unharmed otherwise.

Toby had to support most of Colin's weight; he was conscious--barely-- his face pale again, his eyes dazed. But they moved aside as Madame Meg approached the Hunter with a group of grim, silent goblins behind her.

Abby stopped them. "Wait," she said, and took the spindle from the Hunter's rigid hand. "What are you going to do to him?"

Out of the corner of her eye, she saw Colin straighten, as if he, too, wanted to know.

"Does it matter?" Seth asked. "I don't think he'll be bothering us again." He rubbed his throat, then glanced down at the blood on his hand. Swayed, as if he'd just now realized how close he'd come to dying.

Abby took his arm. "It matters," she said, and tucked the spindle away.

"Let's just say he won't be bothering you again," Madame Meg said. "And that Victor needs an assistant in the kitchens. And that he won't remember a thing once we're done with him."

"He didn't actually kill anyone," Colin ventured to say, his voice cracking.

"Which is why we're not going to actually kill *him*," Madame Meg said. "Boys, whenever you're ready."

The goblins descended upon the hapless Hunter. And Abby turned her back on him and let them do their worst.

Chapter 7

Later, after the wounded had been bandaged and the remnants of the skirmish--it had been more of a skirmish than a battle, Grey opined--had been removed, they gathered at the teahouse again, where Victor served them supper--Matt's wounds had been largely superficial, although Grey had cautioned them to watch for any signs of a concussion; Colin had refused to leave them, and now sat on the floor, his back to the wall--and Abby said, "You'll stay at my house for the rest of the week."

It wasn't really a question, or even a suggestion. She was ready to argue if they refused.

"And for the rest of the Faire, if you want," she added. "It won't be an imposition. Although Colin, I'd suggest that you stay out of my workshop. There's lots of sawdust. And if you were poisoned when the Hunter stabbed you with one of my spindles, I'd hate to see what would happen if you inhaled."

They all considered that for a moment in silence, and then Colin said, "I think we should go with Abby."

Both Seth and Matt looked at Carmen.

"I think we should go with Abby too," she said, and that was the end of any discussion on *that* matter, at least.

By mutual consent on the next day of the Faire, they waited until dark to convene at the teahouse so a much-improved Colin could join them. Colin's performance had netted enough profit to repair the truck *and* buy Carmen a new set of knitting needles (and Seth some spindle making supplies), and Abby had shown Seth the basics of woodturning, which made Carmen jokingly complain that he'd want a lathe next.

Colin had stayed well-away from the workshop, but he hadn't avoided any of them; in fact, he'd taken to spending the day in the house instead of the camper, as if just that small amount of extra space was enough to soothe his frazzled nerves.

He constantly polished his knives, but the others told Abby that was normal, so she didn't pry.

Madame Meg smiled when they all walked through the door. "I wasn't certain you'd come back," she said. "Here, I mean. Did you come to see what we did to your nemesis? Or are you customers this time?"

"Customers," Colin said. "I have a story I want to tell Abby, and anyone else who might want to hear it."

"I love stories," Madame Meg said.

"It's about how we met," Colin said to Carmen's questioning look. "If there are to be rumors, I want the rumors to be truth."

"I'd like to hear the story," Abby said.

"So would we," Grey said from the doorway, and as she stepped into the front room, Toby appeared behind her. Toby, and a whole host of others, dressed in Faire garb, some familiar, others not.

The silence in the room was absolute for a long moment. Colin stood frozen, staring at all of them--the goblins included, Abby noticed, almost buried in the midst of the crowd.

And then she realized that the mundane customers--those last stragglers at the end of the Faire--had disappeared. And that every single person in the room knew what Colin was, and what had happened the weekend before.

And they were all waiting for Colin to speak.

If he had asked them to leave, Abby thought they would have left without a single voiced protest. But instead, he merely nodded, and led the way to one of the far tables.

"I want the truth to be known," he said, simply, and waited until the tables were full before he began to speak, his voice soft, his hands loose at his sides.

"Almost nine years ago, I lay helpless inside a wooden trunk, bound with chains and poisons, held captive by a witch who used my blood for her potions. We hadn't started out as enemies. By the time I trusted her enough to let her know my secret, we'd known each other for three years." He paused. "I lay helpless in that trunk for seven months. For seven months, she let me starve and kept me in the dark. She only opened the trunk to take my blood. And by the seventh month, she'd grown her business in both quantity and fame that I don't think I would have lasted the rest of that year."

The silence was complete. No one coughed; no one fidgeted, although Seth's gaze was locked on his hands as if he were waiting for some damning piece of the story to emerge. Abby remembered what he had told Grey and Toby, and wondered if that was the reason behind his uneasiness.

"One evening in November, a thief broke into the witch's trailer. He opened the trunk, and found me inside. I had just enough strength left to put him in my place--alive--and flee, although I didn't even know where we were. I had my knives, but nothing else." He paused. "*Nothing* else."

Abby saw tears in his eyes.

Carmen reached out her hand. After a moment, Colin took it and then, holding onto her hand as if it were a life jacket and not just a connection to someone else, he took a deep breath and continued the story.

Well Met

Chapter 1

When he found a likely trailer, it seemed to draw him in, promising safety and warmth, even though he suspected he would never be safe and warm again. The door was open; he stumbled inside without checking to make sure the trailer was empty.

Once inside, he wedged himself behind a pile of boxes that sat inside the shower stall--storage, he supposed, but he did not have enough strength to wonder about the contents of the boxes or the occupants of the trailer.

He was asleep before it began to move, and the steady rocking soothed both frazzled nerves and residual panic, now that he was free.

He awoke sometime later to find the boxes gone. Someone had draped a blanket over him; alarm was sluggish to raise its head, but a blanket--and discovery--did not immediately constitute a threat. The heavy blanket draped across the spot where the door did not quite close was problematic, however. It blocked the sunlight, true, but it also--maybe--meant that someone out there knew what he was.

He waited for the panic to rise, but he had no strength left for panic. Cautiously, trying not to make any noise, he pushed himself upright.

And saw the cup--a glass, truly, small, but brimming with the only liquid that would help him recover.

Blood. A few hours old, but still fresh enough to help. They had diluted it a bit with water, but Colin knew that would make no difference; he'd drunk much worse before.

But--was it safe? Did he dare drink it? He picked up the glass and sniffed its contents, straining to detect some sort of drug or poison, but he only smelled blood, nothing more.

He *wanted* to taste it first, but his body had other ideas. The glass was empty before the first rush of healing warmth started to spread through his body. He leaned against the shower stall and closed his eyes.

A door opened. Presumably the one that led to the outside, because Colin smelled exhaust and rain and frying food; the sound of traffic was a loud hum in the background, now that he noticed it. He had been bound for so long that the relative smallness of the shower stall seemed palatial in comparison. He tried to move his legs into a more comfortable position and kicked over the empty glass.

Outside the shower stall, someone drew in a sharp breath. *That* noise had not been overlooked.

"Dammit, Seth," someone muttered--a female voice. And then, a bit louder, as if she realized he could hear her, she said, "If you're awake in there, Seth said we should tell you that we mean you no harm, you are welcome here, and he's working on some sort of protection against the sunlight."

Colin thought about this for a moment. "Windows work," he offered, appalled at how terrible he sounded.

The girl let out a breath. "Good. We weren't sure. Did you--" she paused. "Sorry, I'm not used to this. We left a glass. I heard you knock it over. Did you--"

"Yes," Colin said when she fell silent. And then, belatedly, "Thank you."

"Seth said--" the girl sighed. "He said you wouldn't hurt us. I have a million questions, but--is that true?"

"I--" Colin started to speak, then felt something hot and wet run down his cheeks. Tears. "Yes, it's true. I won't--I won't hurt you."

"We won't hurt you either," the girl was quick to assure him. "Are you--do you want to come out of there? The door outside is closed; it's rather overcast and rainy outside. Seth and Matt are bringing back lunch. They should be back soon."

"Who are *you*?" Colin asked.

"My name is Carmen," the girl told him, and then clearly paused, waiting so he would return the favor.

He spied the case that held his knives lying beside him, hidden by the blanket. Had they opened the case? "My name is Colin," he finally said. "Do you mind if I stay in here for a little while longer? I--" He had to stop to wipe the tears away again.

The blanket covering the door moved. The door, already open a crack, widened. Even though the light hurt his eyes, he could see well enough to identify the owner of the voice. Carmen. She had long, slightly curly black hair, and wore an electric blue t-shirt and worn jeans.

Colin wondered what he looked like, just from the look in her eyes. He found himself shrinking away from her, even though she'd made no move to approach him.

"Someone hurt you very badly," she said, her voice soft.

"What is today's date?" Colin asked.

"November third," Carmen said. "Do you need to know the year as well?"

It was a serious question; he detected no amusement in her tone. "I hope not," he said. "I think--I think it was April when I woke up and found myself locked in that trunk." He rubbed his wrists, unwilling to meet her gaze.

"But I thought vampires were supposed to be--" Carmen stopped. "I'm sorry. I don't want to offend you."

"Do you know who locked me in that trunk?" Colin asked.

"Madame--" Carmen began.

"Don't speak her name, please," Colin said. "She knew what to use to keep me weak. She poisoned me, kept me prisoner--" He closed his eyes, struggling not to remember the agony of endless days of darkness, broken only by the searing light when she opened the trunk to take his blood. He looked down at his arms. They were pockmarked with fading needle tracks. "Used my blood in her potions--"

"How did you escape?" Carmen asked.

"A human broke into the trunk," Colin said. "Looking for something to steal. I--" he hesitated now, knowing what she would think he had done. "I left him in my place." And then, he added, "Alive."

"Seth sensed there was something wrong about *her*," Carmen said. "He insisted we join up at the last show; we don't usually do circuses."

"What do you do?" Colin asked. "I've--I've never *not* been in the circus."

"We travel around the country to Faires," Carmen said, more comfortable now that he'd made no move against her. "Medieval or Renaissance Faires. We get to dress up and pretend we're in Elizabethan England, for the most part. We're actors. Matt is trying to learn how to juggle."

"That's what I do," Colin said, and his hand found the box beside him. He opened it, fearful now that the knives would not be inside, but they were still safely nestled in their places. He pulled up the loose lining of the case and eased out a folded poster; the only one he had left. He had to lean forward to hand her the poster, but she did not hesitate to take it.

His hand shook. Colin sat back against the shower stall before he could do something undignified, like collapse.

Gravely, Carmen opened the poster and studied it closer. "You juggle knives?"

"Yes." All this talking exhausted him; he wanted to curl up under the blanket and sleep for weeks. "These Faires--I've never heard of them."

He fell asleep halfway through Carmen's explanation.

Chapter 2

When he awoke the next time, he heard voices and smelled food; evidently Matt and Seth had returned. Carmen had left the shower door cracked open, although the blanket still blocked most of his view.

The glass had been rescued and refilled. This time, Colin had no qualms about drinking it. There were two things sitting beside the glass; the folded poster, which he replaced within the case's lining, and a small hand mirror.

Colin had wondered how bad he looked; now he knew.

His skin was filthy, pale and tinged with gray under the dirt of long confinement. There were scabbed over sores on his face from the tape and, later, the gag, preventing him from crying out. His eyes were ringed with shadows even now, and sunken; his hair a greasy mess.

He dropped the mirror in his lap. It made no sound, but the conversation outside suddenly ceased.

"We brought you some clothes to try on," a new voice said. "And the shower *does* work, if you'd like to get clean."

"There's a curtain for privacy," Carmen added.

"Do you need help?" a new voice asked, and this one resonated; this voice belonged to the blood he had drunk.

Colin looked up at the shower's knobs. He hadn't tried to stand since he'd collapsed behind the boxes. The blood had helped, but after nearly seven months of starvation and inactivity, he knew a complete recovery would take a while.

"Yes," he said, surprising himself, because he did not intend to ask for help. "Please. I'm--I'm not sure how well I can stand yet."

He didn't want their pity, but he saw none in the gaze of the young man who appeared at the door a moment later. This was Seth; Colin could have named him even without an introduction.

"I'm Seth," Seth said, and offered Colin his hand to help him up.

"I've been drinking your blood," Colin whispered, perilously close to tears again. "Thank you."

"You're welcome," Seth said with a quick smile. "Matt and Carmen have offered to donate as well. Shower first, though?"

The remnants of Colin's clothes were no better, stained and filthy and covered with dried blood. He found it difficult to stand upright and undress at the same time, so Seth helped him with that as well, without a single hint of disgust or complaint. Seth also removed the blanket and Colin's knives from the shower stall before turning on the water.

The first shock of hot water almost brought Colin to his knees. Seth held him up, getting wet in the process, but again, without complaint. And when Colin's legs gave out and he fell against the shower wall, there was another hand holding him up, and a set of hands drying him off, and then--and then, blood.

When he awoke this time, he lay in a bed, fully clothed, with the taste of their blood on his lips.

He opened his eyes. His surroundings seemed clearer now; the light from a lamp beside the bed less likely to sting. When he turned his head, he saw Seth first, asleep on the floor beside the bed, and Matt beside him. Carmen lay on the combination couch/dining room booth; no one stirred when Colin cautiously raised his head.

The case that contained his knives lay at the foot of the bed. Colin slowly sat up and dragged it across the quilt towards him.

It was a large bed, easily big enough for two at the very least. Colin felt guilty that he'd put them out of their sleeping place. He would have been fine on the floor.

Mindful of their sleeping forms, he slipped out of bed and stood on legs that showed no sign of collapse this time. He carefully walked around them without waking them up, holding the knife case to his chest.

He passed a mirror propped up on top of a small chest of drawers and stared at his reflection before continuing into the kitchen. He no longer looked as if he were starving; his skin was no longer quite so pale; quite so gray. But the clothes they'd found for him dwarfed his small frame; he looked like a child.

There was no kitchen table, but there was a chair and a very narrow counter. A tiny refrigerator, a set of cannisters, one marked tea.

There was a kettle on the stove, too. Colin glanced at the others. Did he dare try to make a cup of tea without waking them? He looked at the time on the only clock; it was very early in the morning if he'd read it right. Very early in the morning on his second day of freedom? Or had he slept longer than he thought?

He realized that he felt strange, oddly restless; he knew he should stay inside the trailer, but he also wanted to be outside, unfettered and free. He wanted to see the moon. The stars. Anything.

But unlocking the door *would* wake them, however, so he gently lay the case on the kitchen counter and unlocked it. He hadn't touched his knives since--since *she* locked him away. They almost seemed to leap into his hands.

Juggling had always been a meditation more than mere show, at least for Colin. Despite the fact that his knives could kill him--they were silver--he had never missed. Never once cut himself.

Perhaps it was the risk that made him keep expanding his repertoire; he'd gotten up to a dozen glittering knives at one point before *she* forced him to stop.

Despite the fact that the trailer had very little room to maneuver, Colin took three of the knives and began to juggle, then four, then five, then six before he started to feel a pull in his muscles and fatigue made him cautiously drop back down to four. Despite the fatigue, he felt his tension; the restlessness, drain away. He had not lost his abilities. He still had the means; the talent to make a living. He had not died.

He did not notice that the faint whir of the knives slicing through the air had awakened the others until he saw movement out of the corner of his eye. Years of practice and years of performing in front of an audience had inured him to interruptions, however, and he didn't miss a beat.

"I didn't intend to wake you up," he said. He caught the knives, placed them carefully back in their case, then turned to face Seth, Matt, and Carmen. "I'm sorry."

"No need to apologize," Carmen said quickly. "That was amazing! Are they as sharp as they look?"

"Are they real silver?" Seth asked suspiciously, as if he didn't dare not ask.

"Yes," Colin said. "To both questions." The adrenalin was wearing off now; he wanted to sit down, but he wasn't sure how they would react. Or if he would be able to get back up again.

"Seth told us that silver is deadly to vampires," Matt said cautiously into the silence.

Colin placed one hand on the knives' case. "There would be no challenge, otherwise," he said simply, and hoped they understood. "I can juggle all twelve, but--not right now." When he took a step forward, his knees almost buckled.

Carmen caught his arm and led him to the table. "You need more blood, don't you?" she asked.

Colin sat down. It was either that or fall. "Yes, but not right now," he said. "A cup of tea would be nice, however. I'm sorry--"

"There's no reason to apologize," Matt said, and slid into a seat, leaving Carmen or Seth to make the tea. But Carmen did not seem to mind; she even produced some biscuits that looked a bit like scones.

"Seth told us what you would need," she said. "We don't mind, but we weren't sure how you would react."

The difficult question Colin felt he had to ask hung in the silence. The tea kettle whistled, making him jump. He waited until Carmen had joined them at the table; took a sip of tea to fortify his courage, and asked, "What do you want from me in return?"

They were silent, all three of them, staring at him and then, uncomfortably, looking away.

"We would like you to stay with us," Seth finally said.

"And be the fourth member of our troupe," Carmen told him.

"And teach me how to juggle?" Matt asked. "Obviously, I will never be as good as you, but--"

Colin opened his mouth to answer them, then closed it again. For want of a better thing to do, he took another sip of tea. When he finally found his voice, he was on the verge of tears. "Nothing more than that?"

"Well, we have a million questions, but you don't have to answer all of them," Carmen said.

"I have a million questions too," Colin said, and wondered if he had slipped into some impossibly surreal alternate world. And then, with a sinking heart, he realized what it had to be. "I'm dreaming, aren't I? I'm dreaming." He set the mug down, lest he drop it. "I'm still locked in that trunk, aren't I?" He couldn't bear that thought, and covered his face with his hands. "I--no. I can't. No. No. No!"

"You're not dreaming," Carmen said. "This is real. I promise."

"It can't be real," Colin whispered.

"Why not?" Matt asked, honestly curious, but Colin couldn't answer him; couldn't tell him that they had to be figments of his imagination, because no one had ever offered him what they were offering without some sort of terrible catch.

He was shivering now, in the aftermath of disappointment and fear. He did not want this to be a dream, but it had to be a dream. There was no other alternative.

Carmen's arms enveloped him. He did not think to pull away; to not prolong the agony until someone wrapped a blanket around his shoulders and he found his arms wrapped around Carmen's waist as he sobbed into her lap, as if he was desperate to make sure he never woke up from this wonderful dream.

And it had to be a dream.

After a little while, he realized he lay next to Carmen on the bench, curled up beside her with his head on her lap and the blanket covering his body, still shivering, but at least the tears had stopped. They were talking about him in low voices above his head.

Carmen's hand had settled on his shoulder, drawing him close.

"I don't even want to *begin* to imagine what she did to him," she said, her voice soft. "You saw that poster--that was five years ago. He wasn't like this then."

"She wasn't like that then," Colin murmured. "She was nice, at first. Safe. I needed a safe place. She was the first person I've stayed with who knew what I was."

"It must be difficult to hide from everyone," Seth said.

"I made the mistake of trusting her," Colin whispered.

"It's not a mistake to trust us," Carmen told him. "And we are *definitely* not imaginary."

"How do I know what you say is the truth?" Colin asked. "Why am I sh-shivering?"

"Delayed shock," Seth suggested.

"People *die* from shock!" Carmen said in alarm.

"I am not a person," Colin whispered, and lost himself to darkness before he could hear their reply to that.

Chapter 3

He awoke back in the bed, but this time, Carmen slept beside him, as if to give him comfort even as he slept. Colin tasted blood in the back of his throat again, and knew they all had donated. What he *didn't* know, however, was the truth.

He didn't want them to be figments of his imagination. He wanted them--and all of this--to be true.

Carmen seemed real enough. Colin could hear her heart beating, and, if he concentrated, the blood rushing through her veins. She smelled like jasmine, and a strand of her hair lay across his outstretched hand. And *that* felt like hair. Not a dream.

The blood in the back of his throat tasted like blood, not a dream. The tea had tasted like tea. But he remembered dreaming before, while trapped in the trunk.

"What did you dream of before?" Carmen asked, and Colin realized he'd spoken aloud.

"The past," he said. "Always the past."

"Well, this is the present," Carmen said softly. "And maybe even a little bit of the future." She paused. "Do you know how old you are?"

Colin considered her question carefully. "In actual years? Or how old I was when I was turned into a vampire?"

"Both, I suppose," Carmen said.

"I was sixteen when I was turned into a vampire," Colin said. "I was born on November 3, 1903."

"Happy late birthday, then," Carmen said softly.

"I don't know anything about birthdays," Colin said. "But I'll be happy with freedom as a present, if this is real."

"It's real," Carmen said. "I promise you."

Colin wanted to believe her. With a bit of a shock, he realized that he felt safe here, among them, and it was such an alien feeling that he wasn't at all sure what to think, at first. It had been so long since he'd felt safe. He sighed. Closed his eyes.

After a little while, he heard one of them get up. Heard the muted clatter of pots and pans in the kitchen. Smelled frying bacon.

Carmen groaned. "Bacon *again?*"

"I like bacon," Matt said defensively. "And I'm also cooking your oatmeal."

"You might as well cook me bacon too," Carmen said, and Colin felt a wash of amusement from Matt. Evidently, this was a normal state of affairs. He snuggled deeper into the blankets and tried to banish the question that rose in his mind; tried to ignore the thought that something like this just could not possibly last.

Eventually, he joined them at the table. Eventually, he stopped wondering when he would wake up from this wonderful dream.

Eventually, he realized he'd found both friends and a family, and that his life, for however long this lasted, was finally complete.

End

You can find ALL our books up on our website at:

http://www.writers-exchange.com

All Jennifer's books:

http://www.writers-exchange.com/Jennifer-St-Clair/

all our fantasy novels:

http://www.writers-exchange.com/category/genres/fantasy/

About the Author

Jennifer St. Clair grew up in Southern Ohio and spent most of her childhood in the woods around her home. She wrote her first novel when she was thirteen, and hasn't stopped since. She lives with her ball python, Fester, and two cats, Ash and Rowan.

In her spare time, she crochets, makes cloth dolls, collects antiques, books, and vintage clothing, and takes digital photographs with varying degrees of success.

Her *Beth-Hill series* is set in the area in America that contains many supernatural creatures: Wild Hunt, Vampires, Dragons, Faery and more.

It is part of the Universe that her *Jacob Lane Series*, *Karen Montgomery Series* and vampire trilogy, *The Shadow Series* are set in.

Follow all her books on her author page:

http://www.writers-exchange.com/Jennifer-St-Clair/

If you want to read more about other books by this author, they are listed on the following pages...

A Beth-Hill Novel (Stand Alone Novels)

Are creatures of the night and all manner of extramundane beings drawn to certain locations in the natural world? In the Midwestern village of Beth-Hill located in southern Ohio, the population is made up of its fair share of common citizens...and much more than its share of supernatural residents. Take a walk on the wild side in this unusual place where imagination meets reality.

Blood of Innocents

Ten years ago, Orien, crown prince of the Seleighe, was captured by his mortal enemies, locked in a dungeon and turned into a vampire. Six years into Orien's sentence, the Healer's brother Cullen disobeyed his mistress's orders to kill him and turned him into a vampire instead, thus sealing both their fates for all eternity.

Now both Orien and Cullen are set free. But a secret only Cullen knows lies locked inside his mind, threatening to drive him mad before he can uncover the identity of a traitor- -the very elf who betrayed Orien and left them both to die in darkness.

Publisher: http://www.writers-exchange.com/blood-of-innocents/

Full Moon

Werewolves change into wolves when the moon is full. But Edward's curse only allows him to be *human* when the moon is full.

Alone and despairing, Edward hides himself away from the world. He's scraped out a meager existence for himself for almost a century in the forest he's grown to love and call home. But in the depths of a terrible winter, he stumbles across clues from the life his mother left behind in Faerie. The truth may give him the answers he needs about the source of his birthright... and the curse that holds him captive.

Publisher: http://www.writers-exchange.com/full-moon/

A Beth-Hill Novella: Karen Montgomery Series

Are creatures of the night and all manner of extramundane beings drawn to certain locations in the natural world? In the Midwestern village of Beth-Hill located in southern Ohio, the population is made up of its fair share of common citizens...and much more than its share of supernatural residents. Take a walk on the wild side in this unusual place where imagination meets reality.

Karen Montgomery was an ordinary woman until she stumbled into the extraordinary... A bargain with elves worth its weight in gold. A plague of sinister ladybugs. Rogue vampire hunters, including one who tries to turn over a new leaf--with disastrous consequences. A ghostly huntsmen of the Wild Hunt wishing for redemption. Karen's life will never be the same again.

Book 1: Budget Cuts

Karen Montgomery is used to taking care of the unpleasant jobs no one else wants to deal with. When a shortage of funds forces her to fire fifteen employees from the library, she isn't happy, but the nasty task has to be done and she is, after all, the boss. But Karen finds finishing her task impossible when she can't seem to track down Ivy Bedinghaus, a night clerk she's never actually met. Once she finally does confront Ivy, she's thrust into a centuries-old conflict that makes her previous troubles radically pale in comparison.

Publisher: http://www.writers-exchange.com/budget-cuts/

Book 2: The Secret of Redemption

Karen Montgomery, librarian, finds herself embroiled in another otherworldly adventure...

A member of the Wild Hunt--ghostly myths that aren't so ghostly (or myth-like) anymore--needs help in reconciling who he once was in life and who he is now.

A little girl has gone missing. And the one most likely responsible for her disappearance is the one Karen must prove innocent.

Publisher: http://www.writers-exchange.com/the-secret-of-redemption/

Book 3: Ladybug, Ladybug

An innocent attempt to rid the library of a plague of ladybugs turns sinister when a rogue vampire hunter gets the contract for pest control.

Ivy Bedinghaus, who works for Karen as a night clerk--along with all the vampires in Beth-Hill--are in danger, and their only hope for survival is with the help of Karen, a member of the Wild Hunt, and Russell Moore, a reformed vampire hunter.

Publisher: http://www.writers-exchange.com/ladybug-ladybug/

Book 4: Detour

One wrong turn sends Karen down a road that shouldn't exist, to the site of an old accident and an even older mystery. With reformed vampire hunter Russell Moore's help, Karen finds the key to the mystery. But Russ keeps his own secrets...some of which are deadly.

When old friends from Russ' past come to call, Karen realizes his secrets might just mean his doom. After a terrible incident three years ago, before Karen met him, Russ wants only to live the rest of his life quietly in Beth-Hill. But his secret might not allow him the new lease on life Russ longs for.

Publisher: http://www.writers-exchange.com/detour/

Companion Story: Russ' Story: Capture

Long before Russell Moore ever met supernatural sleuth Karen Montgomery or set foot in Beth-Hill, he was a vampire hunter, possibly the best vampire hunter of all. He brought down whole nests of vampires, caring little about the consequences of his actions. Anyone who lived with or helped the vampires became enemies to be slaughtered.

So what kind of an idiot would capture a ruthless vampire hunter without a conscience and try to reform him?

Ethan Walker was that idiot. Wanting to protect his family, Ethan set out to prove to Russ that vampires weren't all evil, soulless creatures. If Russ would allow himself to witness their lives, see their humanity, surely he and other vampire hunters like him would let them live in peace. *Surely?*

Publisher: http://www.writers-exchange.com/capture/

Secrets When in Shadow Lie

Twelve years ago, Ryan Grey was cursed by a witch to hide a secret. He's lived with the curse of being unable to die permanently, and, over the years he's slowly losing the memory of his past until almost nothing remains.

But now, after a chance meeting with an elf named Zipporah, he discovers the key to unlocking the secret and breaking the curse once and for all...if he can survive the breaking.

Publisher: http://www.writers-exchange.com/secrets-when-in-shadow-lie/

The Dead Who Do Not Sleep

Will Spark only wants a good night's sleep after a night of drinking. Instead, two thugs bang on his door, demanding answers to questions he can't understand. And then they killed him...

Publisher: http://www.writers-exchange.com/the-dead-who-do-not-sleep/

A Beth-Hill Novel: The Abby Duncan Series

Are creatures of the night and all manner of extramundane beings drawn to certain locations in the natural world? In the Midwestern village of Beth-Hill located in southern Ohio, the population is made up of its fair share of common citizens...and much more than its share of supernatural residents. Take a walk on the wild side in this unusual place where imagination meets reality.

Situated in Beth-Hill, where imagination meets reality, is The Rose Emporium, owned by elderly and not-a-little-odd Rose Duncan. The large Victorian house smackdab in the middle of nowhere is a cross between a pawn shop and an antique store that caters to supernatural creatures needing to barter. Rose's twenty-something niece, Abby Duncan, discovers that the world isn't made up of just run-of-the-mill, ordinary humans but an entire spectrum of unusual beings. With her preconceptions about what's normal and what's not turned upside-down, Abby is in for a whole lot of startling truths, mysteries-- about herself and the people and places around her--and danger.

Novella 1: By Any Other Name

Woodturner Abby Duncan decides to sell her spindles at a local Renaissance Festival with only some success. After all, no one really spins their own yarn anymore, do they? While there, she discovers that one of her newfound friends is not what he appears--and his secret is about to get him killed!

Publisher: http://www.writers-exchange.com/by-any-other-name/

Book 2: The Uncrowned Queen

Abby Duncan's elderly Aunt Rose has always been a bit odd. And now she's off on a mysterious trip, leaving Abby behind to run the Rose Emporium, an unusual sort of antique shop. Such an extraordinary store would have been a perfect place for Seth and the others, her friends from the Renaissance Festival, to take a break from traveling between Faires. But when tragedy strikes and Abby and the others discover the true nature of the Rose Emporium, they'll have to travel into Faerie itself before their tightknit group is whole again.

Abby doesn't know much about her family history, but she's about to find out the truth...whether she likes it or not.

Publisher: http://www.writers-exchange.com/the-uncrowned-queen/

Book 3: Coming Soon!

A Beth-Hill Novel: The Shadows Trilogy

Are creatures of the night and all manner of extramundane beings drawn to certain locations in the natural world? In the Midwestern village of Beth-Hill located in southern Ohio, the population is made up of its fair share of common citizens...and much more than its share of supernatural residents. Take a walk on the wild side in this unusual place where imagination meets reality.

A Dreamer dreams the future when the past is not yet laid to rest. Ten years ago, a plague swept across the Seven Kingdoms. Ten years ago, the Queen of Iomar's son was exiled and named the author of the magical plague. Now, in the present, Terrin works to complete his ultimate goal: Control of the Seven Kingdoms using his son's power to supplement his own. But his attempt at dominion meets resistance and the fate of the world rests in the unlikely hands of an exiled prince, a Dreamer, and a vampire...

Book 1: The Prince of Shadows

When Alban's father Terrin appeared at the castle door with a vampire in tow and apologies on his lips, Alban fell under his spell just like everyone else and welcomed him home. But Terrin didn't return to live quietly in his brother's kingdom. He had other plans and, with Alban's untrained powers at his disposal, he begins his ruthless plan to destroy the Seven Kingdoms and rule them all, beginning with his brother's death.

Terrin engineers events to cast the blame on his nephew, Teluride, intending to see the boy executed for his father's murder. But there are those who would thwart Terrin in his mad plan for power, and Alban forms an unlikely alliance with Skade, the reclusive Queen of Iomar, and Terrin's slave, a young vampire with no memory of his name or origins. Although the future looks grim, Alban and the vampire attempt to stop Terrin...and they almost succeed.

A darker history lies at the heart of Terrin's treachery, and only Skade knows the true reason why Terrin would murder his own brother and attempt to destroy both Alban and the vampire to achieve his goals. The Ghost who resides in Skade's mirror--her servant and thrall--holds one of the keys to Terrin's madness. Unfortunately, more than one person wishes for the past to remain the past and the future to hold no shadows of what might have been...

Publisher: http://www.writers-exchange.com/the-prince-of-shadows/

Book 2: Lost In Shadows

Events set in motion ten years ago come to a head as Skade, the reclusive Queen of Iomar, and Nicodemus, who is imprisoned by Skade, struggle to free Alban and the vampire from Terrin's grasp. Old secrets come to light when Skade's exiled son is forced to face his past--or die trying to redeem himself once and for all. Can the crimes of the past truly be forgiven? Only time will tell...and time is running out.

Publisher: http://www.writers-exchange.com/lost-in-shadows/

Book 3: Bound In Shadows

With his power crushed, brother to the king and father to Alban, Terrin is forced to take drastic measures to regain his sons after they are freed and harness the power they possess. But he has an ally inside the healer's house where they are recovering who works to further his plans. The Queen of Iomar, Skade's son, courts redemption to try to save his mother's life, and the vampire who no longer remembers his own name dreams a dream that might save them all...or damn them if success is thwarted.

Publisher: http://www.writers-exchange.com/bound-in-shadows/

A Beth-Hill Novel: Wild Hunt Series

Are creatures of the night and all manner of extramundane beings drawn to certain locations in the natural world? In the Midwestern village of Beth-Hill located in southern Ohio, the population is made up of its fair share of common citizens...and much more than its share of supernatural residents. Take a walk on the wild side in this unusual place where imagination meets reality.

The Wild Hunt roamed the forest outside of Beth-Hill until the Council bound them for a hundred years. Nevertheless, a century of existence has made an indelible mark not easily forgotten for these ghostly myths that are no longer so ghostly or myth-like...

Book 1: Heart's Desire

The Wild Hunt roamed the forest outside of Beth-Hill until the Council bound them for a hundred years--a lifetime for a human but only a passing thought to one such as Gabriel, Master of the Wild Hunt. As the Council's binding draws to a close, old enemies reappear to ensure that the Wild Hunt is bound once more--to a creature much worse than the Council has been.

Publisher: http://www.writers-exchange.com/hearts-desire/

Book 2: Fire and Water

As a young vampire, Erialas Morgan brought his mother back to life with a spell that shouldn't exist, shouldn't have worked...perhaps shouldn't have been performed at all. Desperation and love are his only excuses for doing the unthinkable.

There are others who wish to use that same spell for their own gain--and to destroy the Wild Hunt once and for all. Caught in the middle of a war between the Morgan clan of vampires and their human kin, Erialas turns to the Hunt for help. But even Gabriel, the Master of the Wild Hunt, may not be able to stop the tide of death and destruction once it turns.

Publisher: http://www.writers-exchange.com/fire-and-water/

Book 3: The Lost

Almost sixty years ago, Darkbrook, the only school of magic in the United States, opened its doors to students of decidedly different natures, sending out letters of invitation to the elves, the dragons, and the vampires. The three who responded to the invitation banded together despite their differences but vanished only weeks later along with an entire classroom full of students and their teacher after a field trip gone horribly wrong.

The Wild Hunt has healed and the Hounds have grown closer together, keeping Darkbrook's forest safe and secure for those who live there. Malachi, one of the eldest members of the Wild Hunt, has adapted to Josiah's spell to help him see, but when a demon boy trapped in the body of a human body for sixty years inside the school disrupts the newfound calm, the Hunt--and those they protect--are thrust into a struggle that should have ended long ago when a vampire, an elf, and a dragon vanished into the Mists.

Publisher: http://www.writers-exchange.com/the-lost/

Book 4: A Glint of Silver

Jericho is a vampire who wants is to live away from the Richmond household of vampires led by his ruthless father Connor. When Jericho tries to escape, Connor punishes him and leaves him to die. Tristan is determined to be the one to bring Jericho back, but he can't see him suffer for wanting a normal life. As long as Connor lives, Jericho will never be safe or free. As long as Connor *lives...*

Publisher: http://www.writers-exchange.com/a-glint-of-silver/

Book 5: All That Glitters

As a member of the cruel Morgan Household of vampires, twelve-year-old Arthur Morgan has been abused all his life.

Maya, a water fairy, shows him just how horrible and twisted the household he's grown up is. With her help, and the unexpected help of an adult vampire, Arthur attempts to escape.

Can he become something more than what his father has decreed?

Publisher: http://www.writers-exchange.com/all-that-glitters/

The Chelsea Chronicles

Normally a quiet, serene place, Chelsea Kingdom seems like the perfect location for a centuries' old vampire to blend in and live a normal life, even escape hunters and an angry mob. Unfortunately, his timing couldn't be worse...

Book 1: So You Want to be a Vampire

Chelsea Kingdom is usually a pretty quiet place but recent murders--committed by a vampire--upset the calm. Newcomer to town, Vlad Dhalgren wants only to blend in and live a normal life. He quickly learns that isn't possible, given that other vampires have been hiding in the shadows around the castle--in plain sight--for years.

Despite her lineage, Anna Everett, the crown princess of the Kingdom of Chelsea, isn't a wizard like her father, which means she will never be Queen. She has only one friend, Valerian Moreton--Val--who has secrets he's never shared that could get him *and* Anna killed...

Publisher: http://www.writers-exchange.com/so-you-want-to-be-a-vampire/

Book 2: Transformation

As Anna, crown princess of Chelsea, adjusts to life as a vampire after recent events, Vlad plans for a future he has no real hope to seeing come to pass due to injuries sustained while attempting to save Anna's life. But, as life goes on for Anna and her friend Valerian "Val" Moreton, it changes for others--some of whom are not quite what they seem...

Publisher: http://www.writers-exchange.com/transformation/

You can find ALL our books up on our website at:

http://www.writers-exchange.com

All Jennifer's books:

http://www.writers-exchange.com/Jennifer-St-Clair/

all our fantasy novels:

http://www.writers-exchange.com/category/genres/fantasy/